NORTHERN BEACHES
WRITERS' GROUP

The Northern Beaches Writers' Group is an award-winning writing critique group based in Sydney. We're online at:

northernbeacheswritersgroup.com
facebook.com/northernbeacheswritersgroup

OF BEASTS & BUTTERFLIES

Fairytales reimagined for a modern Australia

edited by

ZENA SHAPTER

Of Beasts & Butterflies

First published in Australia 2019 by
the Northern Beaches Writers' Group, Sydney.

Cover design & internal design by Zena Shapter.

ISBN 978-0-6486802-2-2

Contents

Because stories are magic

Bullets & Butterflies

Phil Burgin

Sarah peered into the darkness hiding the Gippsland landscape that lay just beyond the window of the small plane. Her own ghostly reflection stared back. Rivulets of rain dribbled over the perspex, giving the torches either side of the narrow airstrip an ethereal look. The runway itself, pure black, was an abyss ready to swallow the plane on take off. The pilot turned from his glowing instrument panel and stared at her and Eli, huddled in the adjacent seat.

"I realise your uncle said this was urgent, but we should wait until this storm eases. The winds over the Tasman can get really ugly."

Rain drummed on the roof as the second voice of reason.

Sarah nailed the pilot with a look that left no doubt about her decision. "It's rained for two days. We're not waiting any longer."

"Sarah, are you sure?" asked Eli softly.

"Eli, we're not waiting another twenty-four hours. Every minute we stay here increases the chance of being caught."

Eli covered his face with his hands. "I know, but I got us into this. What if I'm wrong?"

Sarah placed a hand over his. "We chose this path together. We leave together." She looked at the pilot. "Now go."

The pilot gave a rueful shake of the head and pushed forward on the throttle. The single propeller on the aircraft nose responded with a growl as it beat a path through the rain and the small plane lurched forward into the murk. Bumping over small ruts in the surface of the rural airstrip, the plane gathered speed while Sarah and Eli sat silently in the rear. As the runway markers flashed past outside, each breath seemed a little less laboured.

The pilot squinted fiercely through the front window at the configuration of lights at the end of the strip. "Odd," he growled.

"What's odd?" Sarah asked.

"Those two markers. They aren't meant to be there," he said. "Maybe the storm blew them across?"

Sarah leaned forward to investigate as the nose of the plane tentatively started to lift.

The two lights, shining orbs floating in the darkness, sent Sarah's heart racing even before they started to flash, illuminating the metal hulk behind them.

"Holy shit. It's a truck!" the pilot cried.

More lights flared either side.

"Keep going!" Sarah urged.

"Are you crazy?" he yelled. "There's not enough runway." He moved his hand to the throttle and the plane started to decelerate.

"No!" Sarah screamed. "We'll make it." She threw herself forward, jamming both hands over his.

"Let go, you crazy bitch!" he snarled. "There's not..." The pilot slumped backwards, blood pouring from a wound in his head the size of golf ball. Sarah saw the matching bullet hole in the windshield and threw herself into the rear, crashing into Eli.

The dead pilot's fingers dragged the throttle backwards and the nose dropped back onto the airstrip with a thump. Sarah watched in horror as the pilotless plane continued its trajectory towards the line of vehicles blocking her escape. She grabbed Eli's hand and waited for the impact.

⟲⟳

The hiss of the candle announced it was approaching the end of its life. The pool of melted wax threatened to consume the flame, but it struggled on, giving a dull orange tint to the bare wooden walls of the tiny attic secreted in the roof the of North Melbourne terrace.

"Mum, quick, another candle," urged Sarah.

"Shhhh, keep your voice down or you'll wake your father," her mother whispered.

"But I'm not finished." Sarah turned her head back to the fat textbook on the table.

"Sarah, it's late. You need to get some sleep. We both do." Her mother sighed. "I promise I'll get another candle and we'll do more tomorrow night. But it's bedtime."

"I don't think you realise how much there is to learn." Sarah's eyes focused on her Mum momentarily. "Do you know how many species of animals and plants have gone extinct in my lifetime alone?"

Sarah's mother shook her head. "No I don't..."

"More than four hundred native animals, two thousand species of plants and marine animals beyond count." Sarah flipped the book around for her mother. "Look, this book is filled with animals... platypus, numbats, echidna. They're all gone. I so wish I could have seen an echidna."

Sarah's mother started to close the book, when Sarah placed her hands over her mother's.

"Mum, I need to understand how I can save what we have left." Sarah gazed at her mother, eyes bright despite the hour. "And there's magic hidden in books that can show me how but I need your help…"

"Sarah." A sad smile stretched across her mum's tired features. "There isn't much more I can help with. You already know far more than me. More books won't help, you need a teacher. We can't hide up here every night. If your father were to wake we'd both be in huge…"

"You're right," said Sarah firmly.

Sarah's mother hesitated. "About what?"

"I need a teacher. I need to go back to school."

"Don't you say those words aloud. Don't even think them," her mother hissed. "You know school isn't a place for girls anymore."

"I know that. But what if I was a boy?"

Sarah's mother shook her head. "It's too late in the evening for this nonsense. Off to bed."

"Just hear me out," said Sarah. "What if I became a boy, I mean dressed as a boy, cut my hair like a boy, acted like a boy… that's not hard. They're pretty simple creatures."

"Sarah. What you're suggesting goes against the founding order. Men lead, women breed. If you were found out." Her mother shuddered. "I hate to think."

"It could work." Sarah grinned. "You know it could, don't you?"

"I don't know any such thing. Besides what do you think you would do with those?" Her mother pointed at Sarah's chest.

"A bit of binding, loose shirt over the top. No one will know."

"This is not a joke. I can't believe you're even considering this."

Sarah stood, pulled her mother to her feet and held her by the shoulders. She was now the same height as her mother. They often joked about who was taller of the two, but not at this moment. "Why did you continue teaching me all these years? What was the point if you were just waiting to put me into their system when I turned sixteen? I could have spent the last five years sitting around watching my ass get bigger. Would probably make me a better breeder."

"Keep your voice down," she scolded. "The reason I kept teaching was because you were extraordinary at school and I didn't want to waste your talent."

"So don't. Let me do this. Let me take back just a tiny bit of everything the Federation has taken away."

Sarah's mother's shoulders dropped. "Part of me hoped your thirst for knowledge would go away. I'm embarrassed to say that."

Sarah wrapped her slender arms around her mother.

"What about your chores? You won't have time to do them if you're at school." The candle, in its final throes, was losing the battle to keep the darkness at bay.

"Mum." Sarah gave her a broad smile that looked demonic in the dying light. "I'll manage. I'll get up early and stay up late. Whatever it takes."

Sarah's mother nodded. "Whatever it takes."

◦⌒◦

Sarah sat in the quiet of the courtyard adjacent to the school chapel. Dappled light fought its way through the tall scribbly gum at its centre, spilling over her and the book on her lap. Sandstone paving, once patterned and perfect, was uneven in patches, stubby blades of grass fighting their way through the cracks. The red brick wall surrounding the courtyard still bore the scars of a turbulent past, the surface at the far end featuring masonry scored by rows of bullet marks. Sarah, engrossed in the book as she finished the remains of her lunch, failed to notice the quiet approach of Eli, another of her classmates.

"Hey Seth!" Eli cried cheerily.

It took Sarah, still struggling with her male alias, a moment to connect with the greeting. "Oh, hey Eli." She gave the book brief respite as her eyes met Eli's, before returning her focus to the open pages.

"Interesting read, huh." Eli casually tilted the cover enough to see the title. "'The Butterfly Prophecy'. Where did you dig up that one?"

"Library." Sarah's eyes remained in downward trajectory.

"What's it about?"

"Extinction." Sarah raised her eyes. "And how the butterfly is a barometer for our own survival."

"Oh." Eli stood awkwardly, a light breeze ruffling his brown hair. "So you've been here three months, and I'm pretty sure I'm the only other student you've spoken to. Don't you think that's odd?"

"No. I'm here to learn, not make friends, and the only reason I speak to you is because you won't leave me alone. No offense."

Eli laughed. "The reason I keep bugging you is because I've never had anyone in my classes smarter than me. I always thought if that happened I'd be angry, but I'm not. I'm just enjoying the opportunity to talk to someone at the same level."

Sarah cocked her head and peered at Eli. "You do realise how conceited that sounds?"

"What? I was trying to give you a compliment."

"By saying how clever you are?" Sarah smirked, stared at Eli with a raised eyebrow before turning back to her book.

"That came out wrong. I didn't mean," Eli paused. "Look, this is a bit hard, but I actually came over to ask for your help."

Sarah stiffened.

"I wanted to ask if we could study togeth..."

"No." Sarah blurted the word out.

"Wait! Let me finish. I thought we could help each other. You know, use each other's strengths to get better."

"What makes you think I need your help?"

"You probably don't." Eli sagged. "But I need yours. I'm failing science."

"Get a tutor."

"We did," said Eli "I think I knew more than he did."

Sarah shrugged.

"Please. My father is threatening me with military college."

"Why is that my problem?"

"It's not, but once you're in you don't come out. I'll end up a grunt instead of a doctor."

"A doctor? Really? You're failing science." Sarah snorted. "Sorry."

Eli's eye narrowed momentarily. "Look, I know I can get it. I just need the right person to explain it and I think that's you."

"You don't understand. I can't."

"Why not?"

"Sorry, I just can't." Sarah looked at him with sad eyes.

Eli groaned and stamped back through the sandstone courtyard, before he abruptly whirled around and made his way back to Sarah. "I'll fit in with you." He pleaded. "Whatever it takes."

Sarah jolted upright and the book slipped from her lap, hitting the ground with a slap. "What did you say?"

"Whatever it takes." Eli repeated. "And I mean it."

Sarah closed her eyes and sighed. "I can only do lunchtimes."

Eli spun around in celebration. "That's brilliant. You won't regret this. Where should we meet?"

"Here will do fine." Sarah glared at Eli. "Oh, and Eli, don't waste my time. I don't have a lot to spare."

⁓

Sarah's mother steeled herself as the sound of the front door opening and closing echoed up the hall. She rinsed the last plate in the tub of grey water, wiped her hands on her worn apron, and looked up as her husband entered the cramped kitchen. Covered in grimy overalls, his tall frame filled the doorway.

"We expected you hours ago." Her voice was flat. "She's already in bed."

"Got caught at work." He grunted.

She nodded. "You realise it's her birthday."

"Lucy, I'm not a complete idiot."

"I know Bill, I just thought you would try to be here for her birthday. She was really upset."

"There was another failure at the plant." Bill growled. "I can't just leave."

"And you're the only one that can fix it?"

"Lucy, the de-sal plant was built a hundred years ago. No one knows how to fix it. It's held together with whatever we can find." The energy to argue evaporated and his body sagged. The drip of a leaky tap filled the silence.

"She's sixteen now." Bill said softly. "She needs to be registered for harvest…"

"Do not bring that up on her birthday." Lucy said through gritted teeth. "Just don't."

"This won't go away. This is our world now. And the gift will help."

"The gift." Lucy hissed. "You're only interested in the money. You may be comfortable selling our daughter to a government that decides who has children and who doesn't, but I'm not."

"You want to be strung up with the others who defy them?" snapped Bill. "Besides, childbirth needs to be controlled, we don't have the resources to let people do as they please."

"Oh please." Lucy scoffed. "Stop being an apologist for them. If you think they can make a better world with their crazy ideas, you're wrong."

"It's not about better." Bill mumbled. "It's about surviving."

Lucy shook her head. "Your daughter is an amazing, intelligent, strong girl but you're happy to let them crush her. You've no idea how well she is…" Lucy paused.

Bill's eyes narrowed. "Is what? What are you hiding?"

Lucy stuck out her chin. "Your daughter has been going to school… and she is exceptional."

Bill looked stunned. "What? What are you talking about?"

"She's been going to Holy Saviour for the last six months."

"But she's a girl."

"Congratulations, at least you recognise that much."

Bill buried his face his in hands before raising it to glare at Lucy. "This has to stop. You, me, Sarah, the teachers, the principal. They'll execute all of us."

"They won't find…"

"They will." Bill shouted. "Of course they will." Lucy shrank from the contorted face, rigid body and clenched fists. He pushed past her, striding towards the bedrooms at the rear of the house, paused and turned his head. "You put a stop to this immediately or I will."

Lucy burst into tears as he disappeared into the darkened recesses of the house.

Sarah raised her head at the timid knock on the front door. Ignoring it, her attention returned to the open textbook on her bed and she absently brushed away the extra inches of hair that had grown out in the recent months. When the knocking persisted, she sighed, rolled off the bed and made her way to the door. Sarah had the door half open, gave an audible gasp as her hand flew to her mouth. The sight of Eli on the doorstep left her too dazed to open the door any further or slam it shut it. Eli looked Sarah up and down several times before finding his voice.

"Seth? Is that you?" Eli shook his head. "Can't be… Y-you're a girl." Eli stared, open-mouthed, unable to generate another word.

Sarah blinked and came to life. "You can't be here. You have to go." She started to close the door when Eli threw up his hand.

"Stop!" he cried. "I was gutted you left without a word. I thought maybe something awful had happened. I had no idea why you just vanished."

"So now you know." Sarah attempted to close the door again and Eli shoved his foot forward.

"Wait," Eli pleaded. "I don't even know your real name,"

"It doesn't matter," said Sarah. "I don't belong in your world. Just forget about me."

"It's not my world." Eli bristled. "I hate it as much as you. The times we spent together were the only good thing about it. I know this all sounds crazy cause you were a guy and now you're a girl, but in some weird way that actually makes sense."

Sarah felt dizzy and dropped her gaze to the worn stone flagging on the doorstep. Tears welled up as the loss hit her for the first time in months. "Sarah." Blinking away the moisture she raised her head. "My name is Sarah."

Eli stepped back from the door and broke the awkward quiet. "It wouldn't be right for me to come in."

Sarah nodded.

"Walk with me then?"

Sarah scanned the streetscape. "Let's hope the neighbours don't see."

She grabbed a jacket to protect herself from the autumn cool and they walked in silence past the dilapidated cottages that lined the narrow street. At the end of the street was an old, disused cemetery that doubled as a small park. It was overgrown and the rusted iron gate opened with a screech, but it was peaceful.

Eli and Sarah crunched through a carpet of leaves discarded by a nearby flame tree and sat on a bench in an open space between the headstones.

"I turned sixteen a few months backs," said Sarah.

Eli nodded solemnly.

"The next harvest is only a few months away... the thought of being sold to someone to have one child and then be rewarded with sterilisation... it's insane... they're laws made by lunatics and I'd rather die than live by them."

Sarah barely registered Eli's unease.

"We've ruined this place. The sea has eaten our coastline and the desert has almost swallowed everything else because we were so busy being clever, we forgot about the earth... and the earth forgot about us." Sarah leaned in and locked eyes with Eli. "There's magic deep in this earth, magic our ancestors knew of, but we aren't connected to it anymore. You can feel it."

Sarah put her hand on the grass and a contented smile covered her face. She indicated for Eli to do same. "Can you feel it?"

"I think so," Eli said unconvincingly.

"It can heal what we've done but it needs our help." Sarah sighed. "I wanted to help but they won't let me."

"How do you know this stuff?"

"Books. Books no one bothers to read anymore." Sarah watched a pair of white butterflies chase each other between the headstones, darting back and forth until they were lost in the tall grass covering the neglected graves. "I wish I could fly away from this place."

Eli cleared his throat. "Where would you go?'

"New Zealand," Sarah said without hesitation. "Plenty of food, water... freedom."

Eli fixed Sarah with a hard look. "Maybe you can fly away."

"What's that supposed to mean?"

"I have an uncle with a farm in East Gippsland. He's got a small plane that might make it to New Zealand. If we stow away on one of the freight trains that ship food into the city, we could make it to his farm. He would help us."

Sarah processed the information. "He would take me to New Zealand?"

"He did it for my sister when she was fourteen."

Sarah frowned. "You've never mentioned a sister before."

"I haven't seen her for years." Eli's face darkened. "Police think she died in a boating accident."

"Why would he help me?"

"He hates the Federation as much as anyone. He had two daughters." Eli grimaced. "One was harvested but the other took her own life before she came of age."

"God, that's terrible. I can't ask someone who's been through that to risk everything to get me out of the country."

"Us. He would be getting *us* out of the country." Eli's cheeks reddened as an embarrassed grin stretched across his face.

Sarah's stony face, unable to resist, lit up the cemetery with her own bashful smile. "Us." She mulled over the word for a moment. "I like the sound of that."

Sarah wiped the tears streaming down her mother's cheeks, the crying from her own red-rimmed eyes having stopped only moments earlier. Her mother's response was to increase the intensity of her hug to the point of discomfort.

"Mum," Sarah gasped. "I can't breathe."

"Sorry darling," her mum managed between sobs.

"Mum, it's time," said Sarah, which started another round of crying.

"I want to hold you forever."

"You will, Mum," said Sarah and pointed to her mother's heart before pointing to her own. "And you'll be in mine. Always."

Sarah disentangled from her mother's embrace, scooped up a backpack and heaved it onto her shoulders. She threw a rain poncho over the top, opened the front door and walked into the wet, uninviting night.

Lucy stood staring into the murk, minutes after Sarah had disappeared, turning away only when she sensed the presence of someone behind. Bill stood in shadow a little down the hall.

"You couldn't even manage a goodbye?" she asked him.

Bill didn't respond, eyes averted from Lucy's contempt.

"At least she'll be beyond reach soon."

"I need you to understand I did it for all of us," he said softly.

Lucy's heart hammered against her ribcage. "Understand what?"

"They would have been caught anyway."

"Oh my god," Lucy cried. "You told the police they're leaving."

"I had to." Bill moved forward, challenge etched into a face she no longer recognised. "Otherwise both families would live with the consequences for the rest of their lives. As it stands, they'll be brought back unharmed. There'll be penalties of course, but nothing we can't work through as a family."

Lucy doubled over, gasping for air, as her world turned black for a moment. She stood, covered the distance between herself and Bill in three strides and slapped him hard. The sound resonated through the house, her handprint glowing on Bill's cheek. "How could you? This world was killing her and now you've finished her off."

"The Police said they'd bring her ba..."

Lucy hit him again. "You're a fool if you believe that. A coward and a fool." Lucy turned and sprinted from the house "I have to warn her."

"It's too late!" Bill yelled after her.

Soaked within seconds, Lucy ran until her legs were screaming, paused to suck in some huge breaths then charged forward again. The yellow glare of the railyards in the distance beckoned but Lucy couldn't go any further. She bent forward and threw up, her knees buckling underneath her. The noise of shunting trucks travelled through the night and Lucy watched helplessly as a goods train receded into the dark. Bill was right. It was too late.

Lucy wept as she knelt in the road, rain tumbling down, mixing with the tears that streamed down her face.

~·~·~

Sarah watched helplessly as the pilotless plane approached the line of headlights at the end of the runway. Even as the plane's momentum faded, impact with the vehicles seemed inevitable until the plane drifted away from centre, and onto the uneven ground bordering the airstrip. Guided by ghostly hands, it bounced over the rough ground, past the nondescript vans that had formed a blockade, before one of the wheels disappeared into a deep fissure in the ground and its progress came to a shuddering halt, throwing both Sarah and Eli to the floor.

Outside, dark silhouettes surrounded the plane, and the cabin door was wrenched open. Sarah and Eli were dragged from the wreckage, before being separated and placed in the rear of the vans. Light rain drummed on the roof of the van. Muffled radio chatter came from the front. She ran her hands over the side of the windowless van, feeling it, testing it to ensure it was real, not part of a dream turned sour. The engine kicked in and the van rumbled down the airstrip before the hum of the open road took over.

With her personal belongings removed and no external view, Sarah lost track of time. After what seemed like hours, she heard a change in engine note as the van slowed. It transferred to rougher terrain, causing Sarah to lurch about on the seat until the van finally came to a halt. A prolonged silence followed. Finally the rear doors swung opened and the early dawn light invaded her prison. Two masked, military police officers with rifles hanging from their shoulders motioned for Sarah to leave the van. Blinking as she stepped down onto the wet grass of a lush open field, Sarah breathed in the smells of the countryside. A curt hand wave from one of the attending police officers pointed her towards a grove of trees on the other side of the field.

"Not big talkers are you?" Sarah's jibe was met with more silence.

The police made no effort to handcuff Sarah, simply let the

tread of their footsteps over the damp earth behind her serve as a reminder of their presence. The absence of any other sound only fostered her growing sense of disquiet, and when they arrived at the trees she understood why. Secured to the trunk of a thick Bloodwood tree was Eli, hands bound behind him by a length of wire. Two police standing some twenty metres away, were speaking softly to each other, rifles hanging loosely by their side.

Eli lifted his head, tried to smile and failed, his red rimmed eyes a giveaway that he had been crying. "I'm sorry." He sobbed. "This is my fault."

Sarah moved towards him, only to be halted by a rough hand on her shoulder.

"No closer." The policeman grunted. He called to the other two. "Ready?" They nodded and raised their rifles.

"No." Sarah screamed. "Stop. You can't do..." The rest was drowned out by the roar of gunfire.

As his legs went out from under him, Eli's body slumped at an awkward angle, bound hands preventing a dignified end. Sarah fell to her knees, swamped with waves of nausea, unable to breathe. One of the police walked over to Eli and checked for a pulse. Satisfied, he cut the wire around Eli's wrists and lowered the body to the ground.

"You murdered him." Sarah managed between breaths. Pushing herself to her feet, she made her way over to Eli on unsteady legs. There was no attempt to stop her. Dropping to her knees beside Eli, Sarah closed her eyes and gently held one of his still warm hands in hers. She felt an overwhelming desire to dig the fingers of her free hand into the black soil and jolted as an intense energy coursed up her arm, enveloping the two of them.

A world bereft of sound moments ago was now filled with noise – a crow cawing from a mile away, the scratch of a praying mantis crawling along a branch, the patter of hundreds of feet as an army of ants marched across the field. Sarah heard the whoosh of wings upon the air, felt the breeze across her face and opened her eyes as a large black butterfly with brilliant blue stripes landed gently on her hand. She raised her hand to eye level and the butterfly serenely flapped its wings, gazing at Sarah with its dark orb-like eyes. A calmness enveloped Sarah and, as the butterfly launched itself into the air, the tension of the last days, weeks and months fell away.

The butterfly darted away, returned and hovered before her, repeating the sequence. It was calling to her and as it drifted closer, she raised her hands, only they were no longer hands. Sarah saw her own black and blue striped wings, and they lifted her into the sky over the prone bodies of the teenagers and the approaching police. Sarah tested out her new body, tentative at first, but the sensation of the breeze over her wings had Sarah bursting with excitement. The world now seemed so full of vibrant, fresh colours and sparkling sounds.

Diving, rolling and zooming, Sarah explored a freedom unlike anything she had known before and beside her, in all of this, was the other butterfly. The two butterflies buzzed around the heads of the police, now examining the teenage bodies, and they payed scant attention to the two butterflies. As the sun broached the horizon, filling the calm cloudless sky with hues of orange and blue, the butterflies flew ever higher catching the warm updrafts that would carry them a long way from the place that once confined them.

Inspiration: The Lovers Who Became Butterflies

This story was inspired by an East Asian tale called 'The Lovers Who Became Butterflies' as told to Frans Timmermans by Jin Lou. The tale is set in ancient China in a time when girls were not educated at school, and follows the relationship of a young couple that develops as result of a girl who acts in defiance of that rule.

Author: Phil Burgin

Phil Burgin lives on the Northern beaches of Sydney, Australia, with his wife, two children and two dogs. He has a love/hate relationship with writing, which he uses to explore issues such as his current obsession with self-serving autocratic governments. He is envious that both his children are much smarter than he, but keeps this a well-guarded secret. His lucky number is two. Or thirteen. He can't decide.

Scarlet Eats Danger

Azmeena Kelly

Kurt Hunt always sought to find the goodness in people, even though reality often disappointed him. He never stopped believing that the wife beaters, molesters, drunken morons and other dregs of humanity, with whom he dealt on a daily basis, still had some capacity for good inside them. Kurt believed that people weren't born bad, but an unforeseen circumstance simply led them down a twisty turn into vile, wicked ways, and given a chance they still had the capacity to find their way back to goodness.

But occasionally he found himself facing an evil that defied his optimism.

In front of him sat Scarlet, the latest victim of an unnecessary act of violence. She looked more composed than the first time he'd met her. Her hair pulled back into a neat knot above her head, her casual jeans and yellow top were such a contrast to the shredded red dress covered in grass stains and mud she'd worn that night. The clumping streaks of blood, which had clung to her in black gashes a week ago, were still visible across the exposed parts of her body, each one diffused now to a yellowed bruise indicating the passage of time.

She looked up, noticed his stare and gave him a small, crooked smile.

"Thanks for coming in this morning, Scarlet," he said. "I'm Senior Constable Hunt, and you've met Senior Constable Lee?"

Sitting next to her, chatting about her morning commute, was Senior Constable Tessa Lee, the Police Victims of Crime counsellor here to support Scarlet. A halo of frizzy hair surrounded Tessa's round face, and crusted onto the front of her navy shirt were white food smears made by little fingers.

Kurt filled three glasses with water and placed them on the table, signalling to Tessa that he was ready to start. He dragged out the chair opposite Scarlet and sat down.

Scarlet nodded, shifting slightly in her seat as she tucked the edge of her skirt under her knees. "Yes I remember you, Constable Lee, from that night."

"We need to get your account of events from last Friday evening. Are you happy to tell us what happened?" Kurt paused before continuing. "Tessa is here to support you, and we can stop at any time if you need to, okay?"

"Okay, thank you." Scarlet looked over at him. "I just want to get this over with as quickly as possible."

Kurt began recording. "Could you please state your name, occupation and address?"

"My name is Scarlet Thalis, I'm an historian and I live at 245 Victoria Street, Potts Point."

"And can you tell us in your own words, about the events that occurred on Friday 23 April?" he asked.

Scarlet nodded in response. "Yes. It happened so quickly..."

She started tearing up and pulled a scrunched up tissue from her bag, which disintegrated in her hands.

Tessa placed a hand on her arm, giving her a nod of encouragement.

Kurt reached across the table to place a box of tissues in front of her.

"I was out in the city," Scarlet closed her eyes as she thought about the night in question, "with some work friends. It was Gemma's birthday the next day. I asked Wolf along because he was new in town and didn't know a lot of people. We'd been out on a couple of coffee dates that week, nothing major, because I still hadn't decided whether I actually liked him."

"Wolf, you mean Wolfgang Lupin?" asked Kurt.

"Yep, yes that's him." Scarlet opened her eyes and blew her nose.

"So we were at the Three Wise Monkeys on George Street, and I went to the ladies. When I got back my friends were gone, and my bag was gone too. Wolf said he went out for a smoke and when he came back in they'd all left."

"He didn't see them leave?"

Scarlet shrugged. "He said he didn't. I came out of the ladies and they were gone. He said maybe they thought I'd left without them or something."

"Without your handbag?" Tessa asked.

"Yeah, weird right? Maybe they thought I'd left it behind, so Gem would have grabbed it, because she was staying with me that night."

"What did you do then?" questioned Kurt.

"Well I didn't even have my phone on me and I couldn't borrow Wolf's, because I don't actually remember any of my friends' numbers. So I thought I'd walk back home, no big deal."

She stopped and teared up again.

"I'd only met Wolf that week. He seemed like a nice guy; a bit different in a German kind of way, that's all."

"What do you mean?" Kurt folded his arms and leaned in.

"Well, you know, he didn't seem to have a filter. He said whatever was on his mind. I didn't mind it, but some of my friends found him a bit strange, some of the things he talked about. Gemma's a vegan and he said people are apex predators so they can't be vegans, and he almost got into an argument with her about it. I actually thought my friends left because of him."

Kurt furrowed his brows. "Seems a bit unusual, though, doesn't it? That your friends would take your purse and leave without making sure you weren't still there?" He dragged his notebook closer and flipped through the pages. "Perhaps Wolf had something to do with it?"

She looked alarmed. "You don't think he could have made that up, do you?"

"We're still investigating and will look into all possibilities, but you need to tell us in your own words what you remember from that night," said Kurt.

"I told Wolf I was going home, but that he could stay if he wanted, since he'd only just sat down with a new beer. But he sculled his drink in one go and got up to go with me." Scarlet scoffed. "I didn't really want him to come with me, not after the way he had been acting around my friends. Something seemed off about him. He was nice, but maybe he was trying too hard to be nice. And I'm always suspicious of men who are being nice to your face but act differently towards your friends; you know what I mean?" She turned to Tessa, who nodded back.

"But," she continued, "I also thought maybe it was down to him being European, so let him walk along with me for a while." She stopped and gave a small smile. "He was pretty good looking." She turned back to Tessa. "And had a really deep voice, which I love. I remember how his huge shoulders paddled from side to side as he walked, like his chest was a slab of muscle that his joints had to struggle against with every step. Other women would keep checking him out when they walked past us." She stopped and gave a laugh as she remembered something. "Except for this old homeless woman, she hissed at us and scuttled away, maybe she knew something that I didn't?"

Kurt watched Scarlet's face as she spoke. She had been through a significant trauma; marks all over her body reminded him of her struggles from that night. And yet she wasn't behaving entirely as victims in her situation usually acted. She seemed too bold.

"So where did you go after you left the Three Wise Monkeys?"

"We walked towards Park Street and, when we got near Grandma's Closet, Wolf suggested we stop in there to get a quick drink. He said he'd treat me to an espresso martini, so against my better judgement I relented." She picked up her water and took a gulp before continuing. "He told me about his huge family back in Bavaria, how he planned to find a nice girl and live in Sydney permanently. I almost choked on my espresso martini at his words."

"Did you stay long?" Kurt scribbled in his notebook as he spoke.

"No, we left straight after our drinks. We walked along Elizabeth Street towards Hyde Park. Wolf kept talking about how bored he was in Sydney, that if this was Berlin or London there would be life happening at every turn – laughter, music, fighting, blood, people doing all the things people do in a city at night under the light of a full moon..."

"Was there anything unusual about his behaviour? Was he being aggressive or physical in any way?"

"Not really," Scarlet said. "He wanted to hold hands, and even though I wasn't *too* into him, or into public displays of affection for that matter, I let him. And I said a few times that I was fine to go home, that I was a big girl and didn't need him to chaperone me, but he insisted on coming with me."

She stopped. "It was his idea to go into the park, which I wasn't keen on. But he insisted and I don't know why I let him convince me." She absent-mindedly traced a scratch mark along her forearm.

"I was joking with him that he was going to ravish me, and he was laughing, saying that was a good idea. We cut diagonally across from the Park Street entrance and walked over to the canopy of trees in the middle of the park; you know, where the fairy lights are strung through the trees? That used to be my favourite place in Sydney, but I don't think I can go back there ever again."

Kurt nodded, making more notes.

"We sat on a bench under the trees. I remember thinking

how quiet it was in there, other than the screeching bats and an occasional ambulance screaming past. It was so peaceful. He told me how attractive I was, that he hadn't met someone like me before, you know the things boys say to girls in these situations? Then he kissed me, and I'm going to be honest and say that I kissed him back." She reached up and touched her left ear. "Then he nipped my ear. No, not just a nip – one minute he was kissing my neck, then he just went for it. He... bit me. I yelled at him to stop and got up to leave, but he pulled me down, and that's when things went crazy..."

"What do you mean by that?" Kurt looked up from his notebook.

Scarlet shifted in her seat and took a sip of water, keeping her gaze down. "Well, he lost control of himself. I tried to get away, but he was too strong and that's when... something happened." She let out a sigh while shaking her head. "I can't remember what, but I know I tried to run away."

She laid a hand on her forehead. "Maybe I hit my head on something and passed out, because when I woke up, I was lying flat on the ground." She turned her arm to show her bruising. "These marks and scratches were all over me, like an animal had attacked me."

"And what about Wolfgang?" Kurt prompted her.

"He was gone," Scarlet said with an expressionless face.

"And has he been in touch since?" asked Tessa.

"No. It's so strange." Scarlet looked across the table at Kurt. "It's like he'd crawled back under a rock. Maybe he went back to Germany?" She sat back in her chair and crossed her arms.

"Is there anything else you'd like to add?" Tessa asked.

Scarlet shook her head, "No; that's all."

Kurt shifted in his chair as he flipped through his notebook. He looked up at Scarlet. "Thank you, Scarlet, I have one more question. Do you own a dog?"

Scarlet's face went blank and her expression seemed awkward, her eyes shooting up to look directly at Kurt as she spoke. "No, I don't."

"Something doesn't add up." Kurt leant against the interview table balancing his feet against the chair.

Tessa was sitting where she had been during the interview, grimacing as she took a drink of her cold coffee. "It's not uncommon for victims to have memory loss. Give it time; she might remember more in a few weeks."

"No, it's not that. It's more what she was saying – it didn't seem like what you'd expect her to say." He sifted through his notebook. "The CCTV footage from the venues has them at the locations when she said they were there. But we lose them in the park."

"What about the DNA results? Have they come through yet?" Tessa stood to pour the dead coffee down a sink just outside the opened doorway to the room.

"Nah, they're still another week or so off. All we have is the hairs that pathology confirmed as some kind of dog, but we'll need the DNA results to know more. I've put out a missing persons alert for the German guy and we've had to let his consulate know. All we have is her version of the story, so still no real lead on what actually happened." He snapped his book shut and stood up. "I'm going for a walk, need to clear my head."

Surry Hills Police station wasn't too far from where Scarlet and Wolf had been that night, so Kurt decided to retrace their steps. He strolled down Goulburn Street to the Three Wise Monkeys, a bare sad shell of its post-work Friday energy on this Tuesday morning. He stepped back out and retraced their steps along George Street to Grandma's Closet, then continued past its shuttered exterior towards the park.

He walked up the diagonal path at the corner of Park Street toward the middle and gazed up at the canopy of green that Scarlet had described. During the day, it was a dense leafy roof, which cocooned this part of the park from external lights and sounds. He didn't tell Scarlet that this was also his favourite part, and that he often came here to escape the world.

He strolled around each of the benches under the trees, only to stop at the one where Scarlet and Wolf had sat. The forensics team had already scoured clean the area, so he wasn't expecting to find anything new. He walked to the next bench and sat down. There was no evidence or reason to contradict any of what Scarlet had told them. She was the only person who knew what had happened to Wolfgang Lupin, yet couldn't remember.

Or at least, she said that she couldn't remember.

He could easily close this investigation, reaching a reasonable conclusion that Wolfgang had attacked Scarlet in the park and then run away. But there was also nothing to support the argument that Wolfgang was a bad man, not by anyone else's testimony or innuendo; so Kurt wasn't ready to officially label him as one.

He pulled out his notebook and rifled through the notes he had jotted down during the interview. Words and questions stared back, taunting him with more questions. He had spoken to Scarlet's friends and everyone else who had come into contact with her and Wolfgang that night, and no one had said anything contrary to her account. What's more, many of her friends didn't seem to recall Wolfgang, which only made Kurt more curious, more suspicious.

There was one avenue that he hadn't yet explored – the residents of the park itself. Some of the long-term homeless of Sydney often took refuge here, so it was possible one of them had seen or heard something that night. He put his notebook away. Vee would probably know – she'd been a fixture of that part of the park for a long while. Usually, she was hard to miss, wheeling her trolley of possessions around the city. She had a few favourite spots where Kurt would find her reading or having a lie down, her trolley pulled up next to the bench. Anytime he was nearby, he always checked up on her, dropping off a well-appreciated magazine or book.

Kurt walked over to Vee's usual respite, but she wasn't there. He wandered around without any luck, so headed back to the station.

On his way along Oxford Street, however, he bumped into Baz, another homeless man who found comfort in being close to the police station. He greeted Kurt as he walked past.

"Any chance that you've seen Vee around, Baz?" Kurt asked him. "She's not in her usual spot."

"Nah, she ran off, mate. Said something about a monster eating a monster. She's gone off her rocker!"

Kurt crouched down so he was at eye-level with the man. "What did she say?"

Baz's eyes widened in confusion and fear, as if it had been a while since he had to return someone's gaze in such close proximity. "Ah look mate, I don't know; she's mad anyway. Don't know what she said." He stared down at the pavement in silence.

"Do you know where she is now?" Kurt kept his voice calm.

"Well, I haven't seen her since last weekend, when she was flapping around talking about those monsters. Said she was leaving, but didn't have any money. So, dunno how she's going to do that now, aye?" He stopped and scratched his face, staring at Kurt. "I might be able to remember if..."

Kurt gave a low sigh and pulled out his wallet. "Here's a fifty, for a couple of nights in a boarding house, right? If I see you out on the street, then this'll be the last time."

The man snatched up the note and pushed it into his backpack. "She's probably down near the cop-shop somewhere, tucked away in the safest place she can find."

Kurt stood up and hurried back towards the station, zigzagging along each of the side streets leading down towards Goulburn Street, then he cut across the road and walked towards the park next to the station. He kept searching until he could see the familiar overfilled trolley, pushed against a bench in the park.

"Vee? You alright?" Kurt sat down next to her.

She was rifling through the trolley looking for something.

"Vee?"

"You need to go. Go!" She turned to him, eyes wide with fear.

He put a hand on her shoulder and she flinched at his touch. "Vee, are you alright? Do you need help?"

"You can't help me!" She stopped for a moment "Do you have money? Can I have money? I need to go." She shook her head. "We all need to go before the monster eats us."

She pulled various items out of her trolley. Books, clothes, an old style room heater with nowhere to plug it in.

"What are you doing?" he asked

"Need to make money. Do you want to buy something?" She looked from him to the items strewn out in front of them.

Kurt paused, being careful with his words. "Vee, why did you move out of the park? From your usual spot?"

"I told you! There's a monster in there."

He tried a more direct approach. "What did the monster look like?"

"It was a wolf... but there was a girl and then she turned into a wolf right in front of me!" Vee stopped and stared off into the distance before continuing in a whisper. "She ate him!"

Kurt sank back into the bench. "Last weekend?" he managed to mutter.

She nodded.

Kurt felt even more lost. A missing man, a main witness who couldn't remember what happened, and now he had another witness with zero credibility who was telling him there was a wolf in the park. Two wolves.

And the craziest part was that he believed her.

He promised Vee that if she submitted a testimonial, he would to talk to his public housing contact in Brisbane, to find her a new home; then he hurried away.

~～

"So what does this mean? That there's no foreign DNA on her?" Kurt stared down at the lab results, which confirmed what he already suspected.

"That's right," the pathologist said. "The results confirm that only Scarlet Thalis's DNA was found on her injuries. No trace of any foreign DNA. Sometimes, though, it's hard to extract viable DNA from these injuries."

"What about the hairs we found out on the site? Any luck there?"

"Well, they're really interesting," the pathologist leant back in her seat. "We're still doing further analysis because the results are quite surprising. Initially we thought they were dog hairs, but a DNA test shows they're actually from a wolf, Canis lupis of the Germanic genotype." She stopped and chuckled. "But that's not the best part."

Kurt gave a low sigh. "Do I want really want hear the next part?"

"It turns out, Senior Constable, that the wolf hairs are mixed with another kind of predator, and the geneticists here are flipping out because the initial analysis seems to identify them as *thylacine* hair."

"Thylacine? You mean, like a Tasmanian Tiger?"

"Yes! Although they weren't really tigers, they were a type of marsupial – our top predator here in Australia before man came, with a bone crunching bite. Marvellous!"

Kurt rubbed his temple. "Thanks, Liz. But if what you're saying is that I need to somehow write up *a report* on how the Big Bad Wolf just got eaten up by a Tasmanian Tiger, marvellous isn't the word I'd use."

Inspiration: Little Red Riding Hood

The fairy-tale of 'Little Red Riding Hood' inspired 'Scarlet Eats Danger', a retelling that hints at similar perils facing young people today, and one method of dealing with the dangers of sexual predation and innocence lost.

Author: Azmeena Kelly

Azmeena Kelly writes speculative fiction based on human interactions with technology and artificial intelligence, and imagines realities where science and magic merge into one. Azmeena has published a number of short stories online, and in anthologies published by the Northern Beaches Writers Group. Azmeena is working on her first novel, which began its life as part of a novel writing course though Penguin Random House's Writers Academy. Azmeena has a professional background in science, law and change management, and lives on the Northern Beaches of Sydney with her husband, two children and two cats.

Breadcrumbs

Tara Ray

All my life, luck followed me. Whenever I turned around there it was, staring at me. Not everyone around me was so lucky. Growing up in the foster care system, I've seen some bad situations. You might think that growing up in foster care makes me unlucky, but I disagree. People were generally nice to me, I was always clothed and fed, I even had a nice foster brother, at least initially – so I was fortunate compared to many, and I knew without a doubt that things would somehow work out. So I never planned ahead. Instead, I followed the breadcrumbs that led me to the next opportunity, never considered the inevitable prospect that eventually my luck would run dry.

Even in my current situation, kismet prevailed. Unemployed and, to date, with no viable prospects, I received a call out of the blue from an old friend. Her parents would be spending a few months overseas and would I be interested in house sitting? Yes. Yes, I would. The house was one of those modern wonders, all sparkling glass and sharp edges, common in Sydney's Northern Beaches. It was in an older neighbourhood, with stunning harbour and ocean views, where many of the original lots had been subdivided. Consequently, modest Federation bungalows mingled with new homes, featuring floor to ceiling windows and infinity pools. Every parcel of available land had been stretched to accommodate homeowners longing for a glimpse of sparkling sea.

As I reclined on the white chaise-longue flanking the front window, I contemplated my luck. Not bad at all. The next morning, I woke at exactly 6am to the sound of a yappy little dog. Paired with the sunlight spilling in through windows bereft of curtains, I was now fully awake. I peered down at the next house along the street. It was one of the older homes, with a charming white picket fence. The source of the noise, a little terrier, was zipping around the front garden. An elderly hunched-over woman, stringy witch-like white hair hanging past her shoulders, shuffled down the front walk in a dark house coat. She stooped to collect her newspaper, called the dog, and shuffled back inside.

This scene repeated each morning that followed, at precisely 6am I was awakened by feverish yips and yaps, then I watched the old woman shuffle out at snail's pace to retrieve her paper. I didn't pay attention to her house at first. Compared to the new houses on the block, such as the one I currently inhabited, her house was unremarkable. But the more I looked at it, the more enchanted I became. It was a little worn around the edges, but with its red brick, white-painted window frames, and decorative gables, the little Federation bungalow had magnificent bones. I imagined that when it was first built and had more room to breathe, it shimmered in the morning sunlight, basking in the golden glow of the Aussie sun. I also suspected that her view of the harbour was just as magnificent as mine. I loved watching as the morning light turned the sea to liquid silver.

As I jogged through the neighbourhood each morning, I became more and more drawn to the house next door. Sometimes delicious smells drifted from the house, like cinnamon and cloves. I wanted to be closer to it, to go inside.

After a few weeks, I facilitated a meeting. Waking a little earlier than usual, I pulled on my running clothes and jogged out into the rain, passing the house at precisely 6am. As soon as I heard the yaps, I positioned myself directly at the end of the front path as I 'accidentally' turned my ankle and tumbled to the ground.

It actually hurt as I fell with a thud and knocked the wind out of myself. I wasn't entirely sure what would happen after that but, to my surprise, the old woman pulled a whistle from a chain around her neck and blew. The whole neighbourhood would be awake now, I had no doubt.

A burly, barrel-chested man hurtled from one of the adjacent houses. He seemed ready to fight until he took in the scene of me on the ground and the old woman with the whistle. He scooped me up as the old woman instructed him, carried me inside her home, and gently placed put me on her sofa.

I thanked him profusely.

"Any time, darling, anytime," he said. "I am here to serve." He threw back his shoulders and thrust his chin up with such ferocity he should have had a cape fluttering behind him.

I blinked rapidly to suppress an eye roll.

I think he mistook the blinking as fluttering lashes because he looked momentarily surprised, then waggled his eyebrows at me.

After thanking him and showing him to the door, the old

woman murmured, "Careful not to close your cape in the door."

"What's that, Mrs G?" he asked.

"I said, careful not to slip on the floor. It's a bit damp from the rain."

I liked her right away.

Turning to me, Mrs G said, "That was my neighbour, Clive. He has appointed himself as my knight in shining armour. I like to tease him about his gallantry, but I do appreciate the help. I'm not as spry as I once was. How's your ankle feeling, dear? Is there anyone I can call for you?"

"No, thank you. I'm on my own."

She watched me for a second, as if assessing me. "I guess we have that in common, then. Would you like a cup of tea?"

Up close, Mrs G was even more witch-like, complete with a wart at the tip of her long nose. With her slow gait and hunched back, I couldn't have her waiting on me. Instead, I asked her to sit down and keep me company.

After a few minutes of chatting, my eyes fell on a framed wedding photo. "Is that you?" I asked, pointing toward it.

"Oh, yes. That's me and my Edward on our wedding day."

"You look happy," I said. "Look at the way you're smiling at him – you look besotted."

"I was," she said. "I wish he were still with us."

"You must miss him."

"Yes, I do. But it's been fifty years since we lost him, so you get used to things."

"Fifty years? He must have been quite young."

"He was. It was so unexpected. There was an accident. He

loved bush walking and was out near the cliffs at the North Head. Some of those ledges are quite unstable, you know. Always have been. He must have wandered too close to the edge. That was the last we ever saw of him."

"How awful," I said, resting my hand on hers.

Mrs G nodded, rose, and, with shaky hands, lit a candle that filled the room with the scent of sugar and spice. Much to my embarrassment, I drifted off to sleep, right there on a stranger's sofa. I hadn't slept well lately, and here, for some reason, I felt more relaxed than I had in ages.

I awoke to find myself covered in a handmade quilt. Startled, I began to pull myself upright.

"No need to rush off, dear," said Mrs G. "I like the company. Stay as long as you like."

And so I did stay. I visited Mrs G regularly after that and began to help her around the house. Her poor eyesight made it increasingly difficult for her to care for herself and her house, and after my housesitting assignment finished, it made sense for me to stay on with her. Mrs G insisted that I move into her guest bedroom and I began to pick up the slack, noticing where she was struggling and stepping in to help. I scrubbed and dusted from top to bottom. I tidied and shopped and cooked. Clive and I freshened the paint, patched up dings on the walls, and oiled squeaky doors. After we finished, the three of us ate dinner together. It turned out that Clive was alone too, ever since his wife left him for her Pilates instructor. It seemed like fate that the three of us, each a lonely soul, had found each other and forged an unlikely friendship. At night, I sat with Mrs G and read to her for hours.

And then, Hans showed up. I'm not sure how he knew where to find me, but he always had a knack for tracking me down.

Mrs G said, "Of course he should stay here too. He's your family." I had introduced him as my brother, so when Hans kissed me hard on the mouth, Mrs G eyebrows shot up to her forehead.

"Foster brother," I explained. "Not blood relatives."

Other than that unfortunate kiss, Hans was a perfect gentleman around Mrs G. But, as soon as she went to bed, I watched uncomfortably as he appraised the place. He wandered from room to room, picking things up, rummaging through drawers. I knew what he was doing – looking for anything he could pawn.

"Don't even think about it," I told him.

"Ah, come on. Don't tell me you haven't done a little foraging around. That old bat is too blind to notice anything missing anyway."

"Don't. Please, Hans. Don't take anything from her."

Hans shrugged and leaned toward an old oil painting, clearly trying to assess its worth. "Not much around here worth anything anyway. But the house, this land, has got to be worth a fortune."

I shrugged. "Maybe. But it doesn't matter. It's Mrs G's home."

Hans looked at me with a glint in his eye that always resulted in trouble. "Well, she can't have long left. What is she, a hundred and five?"

"No, she's only eighty-five."

Hans snorted. "Only eighty-five. Come on, Gretta. You've been here too long. It sounds like you've been hanging around old folks too long. Next thing you'll be telling me that eighty-five is the new twenty-five."

"No, I'm not saying she's young, but she could have a few more years left."

"Or… we could hurry things along a little. People that age have accidents all the time. Oops, maybe poor Mrs G could have a little fall and hit her head. She's not as steady as she used to be. Nobody would question it."

I blanched. "You couldn't. That would be horrible. Besides, she's my friend."

"I don't know how you can stand to look at her. She's hideous."

"It's what's on the inside that matters," I said.

"'It's what's on the inside that matters,'" Hans mimicked me in a high-pitched, childlike voice. "Listen to you, Little Miss Sunshine."

"Well, listen to you, Big Mr…" I faltered long enough for Hans to smirk before I finished with, "Storm Cloud."

"Good one."

"Oh, shut up," I said. Then I stuck out my tongue at him, which made me feel like we were ten-year-olds again, which then made me even sadder about the man Hans had become.

"Ah, come on now, Gretta. Don't you think you owe me after all I've done for you?" Hans ran his hand over my wrist, gently at first, then his grip tightened.

Back when we were in foster care together, we had been so close. We lived in a rough neighbourhood, and Hans always looked out for me. Later, it became clear that he wanted more from me than I was willing to give. Hans never liked being told 'no'. He never hesitated to take what he wanted. I wasn't like him. I never stole or cheated or lied. For a long time, I tried to look the other way. I thought we could maintain a friendship built of shared childhood experiences, despite Hans' flaws. I tried to see the best in him. Once I realised how brutal he could be, I left. But, somehow, every time I tried to start a new life, he found me.

I gasped in pain as I tried to pull away from Hans' grip. "You're hurting me."

"Look how delicate you are, Gretta. These little wrists of yours – it would be so easy for me to snap them in two. You and Mrs G could use someone strong like me around to help you out."

"We're fine on our own," I said, my eyes welling with tears. "Besides, there's Clive next door. He's always happy to help if we need anything."

"Oh, is he now," Hans said with a sneer. "I would hate for Clive to have an unfortunate accident too."

He released me at last. A bracelet of purple fingerprints blossomed around my wrist.

Hans shook his head, clearly disappointed in me. He pulled out his phone and typed something.

"What are you doing?" I asked, rubbing the tender skin around my wrist.

"Just checking out the real estate prices around here. Can't hurt to stay informed, can it? You just work on getting yourself included in her will and I'll take care of the rest."

"Promise me, promise me that you won't hurt her." I wasn't especially worried about Hans' threat toward Clive. Clive was bigger than Hans and capable of looking after himself. But Mrs G was fragile.

Hans looked up from his phone and gave me one of his dazzling smiles. "Of course, babe. You can trust me."

I should never have trusted him.

A few days later, I returned from my weekly shopping and heard a strange gasping sound coming from the kitchen. I rushed in to find Mrs G leaning against a wall, with Hans around the corner, holding her medication out of reach. Hans was out of Mrs G's line of site. She didn't know he was concealing her pills, but I did. I snatched the pills from Hans and immediately helped Mrs G sit down and swallow them. After leading her to her room for a rest, I turned to Hans.

"How could you?" Heat surged through my body. "You tried to kill her."

With an impassive expression, he said, "I don't know what you're talking about. How was I supposed to know she needed that medication?"

"You've wanted to get rid of her from the moment you arrived."

Hans shrugged.

As long as he was here, Mrs G wasn't safe. Hans would never change. So I took a deep breath and pretended to be calm and rational. "Okay, I supposed it could have been an accident. I'd still like to have a chat. I know a nice path along the cliffs near North Head."

When I returned, alone, Mrs G asked me where Hans was. "He left. I don't think we'll see him again." I fingered the keys to his motor bike in my pocket.

That night, I felt so weary my bones ached. Mrs G. took one look at me and insisted I go to bed with a hot water bottle. Once she had me tucked under the covers, she sat beside me and held my hand. As I stared at the decorative plaster ceiling high above me, everything seemed to swirl. The plaster waratahs bloomed a brilliant red and vines crept to life down the walls. The air felt heavy with cinnamon, sugar, cloves and nutmeg. At that moment, I realised that this was where every step in my life had been leading me. Luck hadn't been following me at all. Rather, I had been following luck.

Sometimes we forge our own destinies and name it luck. Every choice I have made, every star I have wished upon, every breadcrumb I've followed, led me to this place – this enchanted home, the home I've always wanted. And, most importantly, to someone who would hold my hand while I closed my eyes and drifted to sleep.

Inspiration: Hansel & Gretel

In the original fairy tale, Hansel and Gretel are abandoned in the forest by their father and stepmother who can't afford to care for them. Hansel leaves a trail of breadcrumbs to find their way home, but the crumbs are eaten by birds. The children find a cottage in the forest made of gingerbread. It turns out that the gingerbread house is inhabited by a blind witch who wants to eat the children. The witch keeps Hansel in a cage and feeds him to fatten him up. The children ultimately outwit the witch and push her into the oven. They find treasures in the house, which they bring home to their father. Their stepmother has since died. In my version,

Hansel and Gretel (now called Hans and Gretta) are former foster siblings. As in the original story, their parents are unable to care for them. Gretta describes following breadcrumbs to her next opportunities, although her breadcrumbs are figurative. As with the children in the original story, Gretta is drawn to a charming gingerbread-scented house inhabited by an old, nearly-blind woman, who looks like a witch. Unlike the original story, it is Hans rather than the old woman who has malicious intentions. Also, unlike the original story, Gretta and the old woman end up making a happy home together.

Author: Tara Ray

Tara Ray grew up in Austin, Texas, and currently lives in Sydney with her husband, three children, and an ebullient Labrador.

Spellbreaker

Zena Shapter

I snap my laptop shut and leave it on the sunlounger, plod across the verandah's new faux-wood decking and gaze out across the harbour. Sailboats bob at their moorings like frogs on lily pads; neighbours chink evening wine glasses; and a ferry chugs towards the wharf over dull twilight waters. Rich will be home soon. I lean against the railing and wish Mum had never met him. He's as fake as the pathetic brown textures underfoot. Faux wood doesn't snag like real grain. Dimpled knots suggest once-upon-a-time branches. But it's one big deception. Just like the smiles and compliments Rich gives Mum to keep her under his spell.

"I've never met a more amazing woman," he gushed when she agreed he could replace the old wood deck through his handyman side-business. "Have a bath, relax, we'll do the dishes." Then, as soon as she was out of the room. "Clean this mess up, you worthless shits," he told my brother Han and I. "Or there'll be consequences."

He never snaps or yells when Mum's in the house; he saves his breath for when she's gone. "You're pathetic," he usually starts, "you'll never get anywhere in life. How your Mum gave birth to two such losers, I'll never know. Who do you think I am, your bloody godfather? Get working!"

I've tried to tell Mum but she never believes me, thinks I'm jealous. I gaze at the late afternoon sky as if it might bring her home early from Singapore, cancel her latest conference, regional meeting or strategy whatever. "Be nice to Rich," she told Han and I before she flew out. "He's taken on a lot, coming to live with the three of us."

If they marry, I don't know what Han and I would do. Run away?

No. After Dad died, Mum cried all the time – while cooking dinner, loading the washing machine, standing right here in the dark of night, searching for some twinkle of starlight to see her through. I couldn't make her that way again. Exams, university, escape – subtlety is my only option.

Behind me, paws pad across the deck. Shit, did I leave the French doors open? George stops at my heels, panting as pugs do, his eyes glistening like dew on a dawn-wet spiderweb. He smells like he needs a bath. "Back inside, George," I tell him, pointing at the doors. "You know Rich doesn't like you out here." George doesn't move, so I pick him up. Rich can be scary when he's angry. "Wow, George, you're getting heavy. All the Wagyu Rich feeds you?"

Footsteps.

Too heavy to be my brother.

Work boots stomp across kitchen tiles.

Rich.

He yanks the French doors open with so much force they generate an airstream.

"I was just brin…"

"What the fuck are you doing with my dog?" Rich strides over. "Were you about to… throw him off?"

"What? No, of course not, I…"

He wrestles George from my arms, storms back across the deck, drops George onto the kitchen tiles and slams the doors shut. "You know, I really try with you kids." He walks back towards me, shaking his head. "But you just won't do as you're told, will you?"

"No, I…"

"What's my dog ever done to you, eh? Nothing, that's what. You're a coward, toying with him like that. How would you feel if I did the same to you, huh?" He crouches, grabs me around the thighs and lifts, tilting me towards the railings.

"Put me down, Rich!" I hold onto his shoulders. What's he doing? "Let me go."

"Not much fun, is it?" He tilts me further.

My heartbeat quickens. "Stop it!" I manage, my lungs tightening. Is he serious? "I never did anything to George!"

"Only because I stopped you." He lifts higher, tilts more, grins while staring at the driveway beneath us. "How do you think George felt?"

"Please, Rich." My voice cracks. Tears well. If Rich were to let go, I'd fall five metres onto concrete.

More tilting.

I scream.

Higher.

I slip from his hold and slam into the railings, grasp at its glass rim for leverage. It's too smooth.

The French doors fling open. "Put her down!" Han demands. My brother's home too? "Now!"

Rich lowers me slightly. "Well aren't you the big man," he sneers at Han, "barking orders. When did you grow up?"

Han strides over. "The minute I saw you dangling my sister over the driveway. Now put her down, or I'll get my mates to help you."

Three of Han's mates stand in the kitchen, arms crossed, glaring. Fifteen years old, they're each as tall as Rich; muscles not as thick, but they have the numbers.

Rich lowers me to the ground.

I push him away and run to my brother.

"Come on, Grets." He snatches up my laptop, puts his arm around me, and guides me back inside. "We're out of here." He gestures for his mates to bring his school bag, open on the kitchen counter.

I'm shaking so much I hardly notice a ghostly shiver run through me.

We stop by my bedroom for my jacket, keys, wallet.

"Actually, pack a few things." Han points at my sports bag. "Warm clothes."

Han's mates guard my doorway while he disappears into his bedroom.

I empty my bag and fill it with essentials.

Han reappears with his school bag so packed it bulges, then leads me out the front door. Are we running away?

We follow his mates onto the coastal path, around to North Harbour Reserve, then cut across to the harbour walk towards Forty Baskets Beach, passing through the dusk-lit bush. Trees darken the twilight with tangled branches as black as burnt bones. Ferns sprout and reach over our path as if to push us back. Magpies gargle in the shadows like they're casting a spell. A salty breeze sniffs around my neck.

"Where are we going?" I ask Han.

"To the Sugar House."

"The what?"

"Don't worry, my mate Cal runs the place. It's safe. You'll like it."

His mates chuckle and exchange glances as if sharing some secret.

Han puts his arm around me. "Anywhere's better than there, right?"

I smile in agreement but it doesn't feel right. Han and I haven't talked in a while. He's only home when Rich says he has to be, for weekday evening meals, and to sleep. Two afternoons a week I thought he went to soccer practice, or cricket. Now I think about it, he hasn't played a Saturday game in a long time. Has he dropped out?

Up ahead, the golden-grey gleam of sand and still harbour waters gleam through the trees. Families mill about the beachside barbecues as ants over dropped gingerbread.

Han veers off. "We're here." He points through the bushes.

A trail of white pebbles leads to a tall stone wall, overgrown with so much ivy it's almost invisible amid the shaded greenery. A decaying wooden gate hangs off its hinges to slant across a dark gap. Han and his mates speed up, even jog towards it. They raise up the gate's fraying edges to ease it open, hold it ajar for me. I grasp onto it for balance as I squeeze through. One side is furred with green moss, splinters – real wood with furrowed grain. The other side is covered with pinned wrappers from sweets and biscuits, some paper and torn, others plastic and faded: Caramello Koalas, Violet Crumbles, Cherry Ripes, Jaffas, Mint Slices and Tim Tams. A breeze plays with crinkles and loose ends, fluttering them like a warning. What is this place?

"Come on, Grets," Han beckons, heading into an unkempt garden, overshadowed by the thick canopy of a large Moreton Bay fig tree. Its gloomy branches clutch at the air like the crooked fingers of an ancient witch. Its high roots hump with disdain. Wind chimes made from broken glass bottles dangle down and sway.

Beyond it, a derelict weatherboard house is also covered from roof to foundations in wrappers. A honeyed smoky aroma seeps out its backdoor. Han hurries towards it.

I follow, stumbling over knee-high weeds. "What's with all the wrappers?" I ask Han.

"That's what we do at the Sugar House, sis – take a chill, eat snacks. You'll see." He tugs the backdoor towards him and it creaks open like a cackle. A soft steady musical beat drifts into the evening chill. The orange glow of a warm fireplace welcomes us as we step inside. The air is hazy. I didn't know people still smoked, yet several teens lounge on beanbags and suck on lit rollies. Their smoke doesn't smell like tobacco though; instead it carries the sweetness of boiling caramel, maple syrup on hot pancakes, lemon ginger tea...

"Hansel, my man!" says a guy wearing boardies and nothing else. Lank blond hair drapes across his face like a half-drawn curtain. He holds up his hand but doesn't move, barely opens his eyes.

Han dumps his school bag, then takes the guy's hand to shake, grip and bump. "Grets, this cool dude is Cal. He'll take care of us." He slumps into the beanbag next to Cal and sighs like he's finally home. Cal passes him his rollie and Han takes a drag. "Cal lives here, the lucky bugger."

Cal gestures at the beanbag next to Han. "Pleased to meet you, Grets. Take a chill."

I sit, rest my bag beside me, then fight against the beanbag's yielding form, trying to keep myself upright. It's a pointless exercise, so I fight my wariness instead – Han said we'd be safe here. I slump into the squishy material and take some deep syrupy breaths to calm myself. My head sways. Probably all the stress of what happened with Rich. Did he really just tilt me over the driveway? The thought of it should fire me up – how dare he even touch me! Somehow, though, it's more of a curiosity. What on Earth made him think that a good idea?

Across the room, Han's mates slink onto the floor, take out rolling papers.

It's so nice and warm in here. The perfect temperature.

"Did you bring snacks?" Cal asks Han.

Han passes Cal his rollie, opens up his bag. From underneath his clothes he pulls out share-packets of chips, biscuits and slabs of chocolate.

Cal smiles. "My man. Snacks and decoration in one."

Han passes them over, along with a clip of banknotes in every colour – pink, blue, red, yellow... and green. Where did he get all that money?

I open my mouth to ask, then realise I can't be bothered.

Everyone else is rolling, lighting, inhaling and leaning back to unwind. I need a break too – from everything, to give me some perspective. I cough on the smoky air, then nestle into my beanbag, close my eyes and slow my breathing. The last thing I want is to upset Mum. At the same time, we can't go on like this. Mum, Han and I need to be a family again, just the three of us. I grin at the thought, glance around the dark room, faces lit by flickering firelight, happy faces. Han and I could also be happy here. It's nice here. Better than there.

I close my eyes again, inhale softly and drift. Sleep finds me.

In the middle of the night, an owl hoots from the fig tree and wakes me. Glass wind chimes tinkle as delicate as the laughter of fairies. My stomach grumbles, starving. Han is asleep next to me, his mouth open, drool sliding. Crumbs dust his lips. A packet of chilli-flavour chips lies open on his lap, his hand still inside it. I crawl over, stuff my mouth with chips then spy an unopened Mars bar on the floor.

Next morning I wake on my front lying across Han's legs, the last of the Mars bar still in my hand, Han trying to retrieve his legs from under me.

"Grets, what're you doing?" he mumbles. "Shit." His chip packet is on the floor, a cascade of deep-fried potato slices flows from his lap. He sits up, eats chips as he finds them.

"What am *I* doing?" I move back onto my heels, slowly because everything aches. "What are *you* doing?" I snap, tensing. "How often do you come here, Han? That stuff you're smoking, it isn't tobacco." It can't be, not after what its smoke has just done to me. "We're not 'safe' here!"

"Chill, sis, it's all good."

"Good? Drugs aren't 'good', Han, you know that." The blurry haze of last night slowly clears. "Is this why you quit soccer, cricket? How long have you been coming here?"

"Just chill, will you?"

"Chill?" Is he still high?

Cal stirs. "Quit the noise." He nudges the girl across from him with his foot. "Jen, put another log on."

It is a bit brisk.

Jen mumbles something, curls her body away so he can't reach her, goes back to sleep.

I'm nearer anyway, so crawl to the fireplace, haul a log off a nearby stack and prod it into glowing embers, stirring flames.

"It's fucking freezing." Cal shivers, eyes still closed.

"Morning to you too," I mutter sarcastically, slumping back into my beanbag.

"Morning?" Cal sits up, squints against the harsh light streaming in through the window. "Shit, man, you gotta go," he tells Han. "We got a delivery this morning. You know you can't be here when the witch comes."

Did he say 'witch'?

Han seems to understand, stumbles to his feet. "Grets, we gotta go a while but we can come back."

"Why?" I ease myself to standing.

"Because Mum's not home until Tuesday and we need somewhere to crash until then." He points at my bag. "Just leave that here."

"No I mean why only us?" I gesture at Han's mates, the other teens, all still sleeping.

"I dunno – coz we're underage or something?" He shrugs. "Whatever Cal says, man, just go with it."

Cal pushes his hair off his face, hand shaking with nerves. "Nah, man, I don't make those rules, the witch does. And she's right, your mates gotta go too, remember?"

A key in the front door; it glides open as if haunted.

"Ah shit," Cal sounds as if he's about to cry. "I'm gonna be in so much trouble."

Footsteps.

Too heavy to be another teen.

Work boots stomp across floorboards.

Surely not?

I rub my eyes, yet there stands Rich in the lounge-room doorway.

"Hey, sorry man," Cal says, flicking his hair aside. "I know you said never to let them see you here, and I know it's delivery day; but shit man, this stuff's so dope we slept in."

Rich glares at me, then Han, then Cal again. Several zip-lock bags of dried leaves dangle in his hands. Is that what these teens are smoking? Is Rich their... drug dealer?

Cal holds a hand out for the zip-lock bags. "Wanna take a chill, witch?"

Witch? He means Rich.

"Ha!" I chuckle, a little giddy with the truth. "I don't believe it." I also easily believe it. "You're a worthless piece of shit – a drug dealer!" More than that. "You knew Han was coming here, taking this stuff. But, what, you didn't want him seeing you here as his supplier, in case he told Mum? Such an ass. Coward."

Rich clenches his fists. "You can't speak to me like that here!" He steps towards me. "Here I'm someone else and you will respect me." He drops the bags in Cal's lap and lunges at me.

But I'll never let him touch me again. I reach into the fireplace and grab my log by its cool end, fend Rich off with the end now in flames.

Unable to stop in time, he lurches straight into it. Honey flashes scorch his face, caramel flames lash into his hair. He cries out in pain, slaps his head to put out the fire, yelps each time he touches melting skin. Finally he understands the power of real wood.

"Stay away from us! Or there'll be consequences!" I drop the log, snatch up my bag and grab Han's arm. "Quick!" I pull him out the backdoor and run, dragging him past the fig tree. He almost trips on weeds, but at least the back gate is still ajar. We squeeze through and follow the white pebbles to the path. Morning barely lights our way through the bush, but I don't stop. I need to get Han away from that place. Once we're home, I'll have the locks changed, secure the driveway gates and reset the footpath keypad code. If Rich still tries to get in, I'll call the police. There's no choice in the matter now, Rich has to go. Mum will just have to cope.

Panting, we race away from Forty Baskets, around North Harbour Reserve, up the hill, up our driveway. I fumble in my bag for my house key, but the door flings open.

Rich?

Mum. Home… early. She wraps her arms around me and Han, and we waddle inside together. "Thank god, where have you been?" She's been crying. "I phoned last night, Rich said you'd walked out. I got here fifteen minutes ago to find the place empty. What's been going on?"

I reach behind us, shut the door, and tap our keypad to secure the gates. "Call a locksmith and I'll explain."

She frowns, hesitates.

So I take her phone out of her hands, search Google and call a locksmith myself. I don't want to see her in pain, but I'm ready now to break the spell Rich has cast over my entire family. He won't touch any of us again.

George sniffs up round me as I dial. Probably he can smell the singe of burnt flesh.

Inspiration: Hansel & Gretel

'Spellbreaker' is inspired by 'Hansel & Gretel', a fairytale originally recorded by the Brothers Grimm in 1812. It's found in many variants across many cultures, including the Doctor Who Expanded Universe (as 'The Gingerbread Trap'). It has been adapted for opera, television and film. Much like the original, my modern-day adaptation features two neglected children seeking refuge in a house covered in sweets. Although trapped by the house's enticements, they defeat an evil 'witch' with fire and return home to be welcomed by a remorseful parent.

Of Beasts & Butterflies

Author: Zena Shapter

Zena Shapter writes from a castle in a flying city hidden by a thundercloud. Her writing reaches across ages and genre into the heart of storytelling. She's won over a dozen national writing competitions – including a Ditmar Award, the Glen Miles Short Story Prize and the Australasian Horror Writers' Association Award for Short Fiction. Her short work has appeared in the Hugo-nominated 'Sci Phi Journal', 'Midnight Echo' (as well as their Australian Shadows Awarded 'best of' anthology), 'Antipodean SF' and Award-Winning Australian Writing (twice). Reviewer for Tangent Online Lillian Csernica has referred to her as a writer who "deserves your attention". She's the author of 'Towards White' (IFWG 2017) and co-author of 'Into Tordon' (MidnightSun 2016 / Scholastic Distribution). She's a movie buff, keen traveller, story nerd, and inclusive creativity advocate, who's founded community creativity projects for writers such as the 'Art & Words Project' and the award-winning Northern Beaches Writers' Group. She's also a writing mentor, editor, book creator, HSC English tutor, Service NSW Creative Kids Provider, and short story judge. Her work is represented by the Donald Maass Agency in New York. Find her online via every major social media platform and zenashapter.com

Mermaids

Joanna Mawson-Lee

The waves were silky smooth, softly rising and falling under a slate grey sky as surfers glided upon them, cutting through the soft fabric of the ocean, far removed from the throngs of people walking up and down Manly promenade. Some surfers just sat on their boards, slick black figures of restrained momentum, waiting, with legs dangling like puppets.

Alana breathed in deeply, bobbing up and down over the waves, almost bubbling over with excitement as she waited for her next ride. Today was her eighteenth birthday and finally it was her turn to have a big party, just like all three of her sisters before her. Her whole family was out for their Saturday morning surf, something they tried not to miss since their mother had died five years ago. It was their way of feeling closer to her, among the waves, sensing her presence.

"I've got this one, it's mine!" yelled Freya, her sister closest in age. With a determined grin and a shock of curly pink hair, she moved swiftly to overtake a wave, her body primed ready to spring to her feet.

Summer, Alana's eldest sister was far out among the breakers with the more experienced surfers, her lithe, strong body glistening like a young seal in her black wetsuit.

Alana's other sister, Bethany, was chatting up the boys as they waited on their surfboards, flashing her dark green eyes and tossing her long blonde hair as she leant across her board to drape herself over a young surfer's unsuspecting shoulder.

Alana chuckled, she was not sure what Bethany found so interesting in these sun-drenched surfers, most of whom they had known since childhood. One of them, her best friend Slater, was gesticulating wildly for her to paddle further out and join him, but she waved casually back and shook her head. Before the chaos of party preparations took hold, Alana wanted some quiet time on the waves, alone with her mum; how proud her mum must be, somewhere in time and space, of her turning eighteen. Alana imagined her sitting beside her on some ethereal surfboard, utterly free and at one with the waves. Was it just imagination or her mother's spirit? She would never know, but she could feel her love and that's all that mattered.

Tears stung her eyes, mixing with the salty water. "I love you mum," she whispered, brushing away her tears, then paddling fiercely to catch the next wave. The board lifted beneath her, catching on the wave as she leapt to her feet. It propelled her forward in a gentle hold, carrying her safely to shore.

Wading out of the water, her legs wobbly and her cheeks flushed, she waved goodbye to her sisters and headed towards her bicycle, padlocked nearby. Soon she was cycling along the boardwalk, her surfboard clamped to the side of her bike.

"See you later, Dad!" she yelled, as she passed her father, waxing his board alongside a few of his old surfing mates, his thick mane of hair like an old sea lion's.

He looked up and laughed, "Hey, slow down birthday girl!"

She grinned and shook her head, catching his wistful look as she cycled on her way. She knew he would be thinking of her mother; she never got tired of hearing him say that she had the same determined little figure and intense blue eyes.

Jed watched Alana slowly disappear from sight and sighed to himself. His girls were all grown up now, his 'little mermaids' as he often called them, for their whole family lived and breathed the ocean. In his prime, they had called him a 'legend', surfing the monster waves of Mavericks in California. He had trained for weeks at a time, just so he could hold his breath long enough to survive the crushing weight of those enormous waves.

Then suddenly, on one of those trips, his vibrant, fearless wife had lacerated her leg after a wave dumped her onto some treacherous rocks. The whole family had watched on helplessly, numb with shock, as the wound had quickly become infected and septicaemia had taken its dreaded hold.

His wife's death had crushed him more than those giant waves had ever done. Time and again, it had sucked him down into the depths of grief, but each time he had resurfaced, forcing himself to keep moving, loving his girls and fighting against it. His passion for life, the joy and laughter of his girls, and the memories they all shared, had been the foundation upon which he had built their new life.

"Life is good," he boomed to a wiry, grey-haired surfer standing next to him, shaking off his pensive mood. "That's my youngest, did you see her? She's eighteen today, can you believe it? Four amazing daughters, and I was loved by their amazing mother, what more could a man ask of life? And best of all, plenty more waves to surf!"

"Congrats, mate. Yup, a good day for a surf, bro!" his friend said casually, picking up his board, intent on the waves.

They lumbered across the sand and crashed into the shallows, scattering the terrified young nippers messing around on their boards before them, as they launched themselves onto their boards in unison, powerful arms propelling them over the breakers.

Each of the sisters had picked one of the big hotels close to the ocean for their eighteenths, but Alana had chosen St Pat's, as it was known to the locals, sitting high up on the hill above Manly, overlooking the Tasman Sea. At night it was like a fairy-tale palace, lit up brightly with golden lights. It was no longer a seminary, no boys studied there to become priests, instead business students roamed around the grounds. Still, it was a magical place to Alana, especially since its century-old, heritage buildings could be hired out for parties like hers.

She stood at the entrance to the Great Hall, which stretched out towards a large balcony overlooking the ocean, with beautiful drapes hung high across the ceiling beams. Her whole family were out in force. By her side, her father looked magnificent in a dark purple tuxedo with his thick golden hair tumbling over his shoulders, his huge physique instantly swamping anyone who made the mistake of standing next to him. Bethany and Summer both shimmered in beautiful gowns, the colours of the sea, and Freya was wearing tight red trousers, platform shoes and a bright pink top, to go with her hair. Alana burst with pride, what a family!

She peered around the corner into the kitchen, where waiters were preparing to provide a full silver service, noticing with satisfaction that the jazz band she had hired were just setting up beside the dance floor. Her father had initially raised one large, bushy eyebrow at her request and peered quizzically at his youngest, but he had eventually given her free reign. After years of surfing parties and a punk-rock sister, Alana yearned for the elegance of an era long gone. She cast a wry eye at her father, bellowing his enthusiasm across the floor at some old surfing mate who he had just spotted.

After dinner, while musicians tuned their instruments, and plates were taken away, people rose from their chairs to circulate or head towards the dance floor. Running her hands over her silky, blush-coloured gown, Alana sighed with satisfaction. Everything was perfect, nothing had gone wrong; the waiters and waitresses in their black and white uniforms looked the epitome of professional, the roses were the exact colour she had ordered, the best champagne sparkled in the crystal cut glasses, and the pile of gifts on a central table beckoned enticingly.

All around her were the familiar faces of family and friends, a tight-knit surfing community. Slater's lean youthful form, always ready to dance, moved towards her expectantly with a huge smile on his face. No doubt he would try to kiss her again, but as he liked kissing girls in general, she wasn't too worried about hurting his feelings and refusing him yet again.

Everything was perfect, so why was she feeling slightly flat?

Just as she was wondering whether it was possible that she could actually be bored at her own birthday party, she noticed a flurry of activity and a group of latecomers arriving. The girls started to flutter and even the boys seemed curious. Then the new arrivals, a group of effortlessly stylish young men and women walked casually across the room, to greet her sister Summer, who must have invited them to the after-party.

"Who are they?" Alana asked Freya, who was sitting beside her, chatting to their mother's best friend.

"Ah, I think those are Summer's friends from university."

And before she knew what was happening, Summer was introducing her to the group, the birthday girl of course, and Alana suddenly found herself shaking hands with the guys and kissing the cheeks of the girls, unable to say even a word to these glamorous beings. Bethany rushed over, her blonde hair shimmering, her eyes sparkling with interest, and Alana found herself pushed into the background.

Then the hum of the party, the voices of her sisters, the sound of the band, all faded into the background, as she saw his face for the first time.

He must have entered the party after his friends, so they were not formally introduced. But there he was, this tall, dark and athletic man who was, more importantly, thought Alana, perfectly at ease in a tuxedo, unlike some of the other young men, who looked as if they had been wedged into theirs on pain of death.

For the rest of the evening, she talked distractedly to family and friends, danced to the music, drank more than was good for her, opened gifts, and kissed so many cheeks, that she began to feel like a 'thank you for coming' smiling robot. But all the time, moving around the room, like a blip on her radar, there he was.

It was only when his group started to pick up their bags and jackets, preparing to leave, that she suddenly panicked. She had not even spoken to him, maybe she would never see him again. Somehow, possibly in a parallel universe, some version of herself found the courage to rush up to him, and clumsily blurt out.

"Hi, I'm the birthday girl, Alana, we didn't get a chance to say hi."

He turned to gaze at her with dark brown eyes, and smiled.

"Hi, I'm Caspian. Sorry, happy birthday. I missed out on the introductions, didn't I? And we've been having such a great time that I didn't get the chance to come over."

"Yes, I know," she said rather lamely.

He glanced at her, thoughtfully. "Look, a bunch of us are hiring a private yacht next weekend; we're going to cruise around the harbour and wallow in luxury for an afternoon. If you and your sisters wanted to join us? You'd have to chip in with the hire obviously, but it would be an amazing day."

"Oh yes, thank you, I'd love to!" she said, opening like a flower at his friendliness.

She tried not to think about the minor detail that she only had fifty dollars until the next payday from her job at the café, after buying her rather expensive dress for the party.

"Great, I'll see you then! Turn up at the Spit Wharf, you won't be able to miss us. Don't forget to bring your swimmers, you can swim, can't you?"

"Yes, I can swim," she said simply.

And then he was gone, without even asking for her phone number.

She wondered at herself – if any other boy had asked her if she could swim, she would have mocked him derisively, listing all the surfing trophies that she and her sisters had collected over the years.

The next day, Alana desperately tried to persuade Summer that an expensive party on a private yacht was exactly what she wanted to spend her hard earned savings on, even though Summer already had a boyfriend – they were practically engaged – and was saving up for a big trip around the world with him, to all the best surfing destinations.

"Sorry, Alana, but Caspian, I mean he's good-looking and intelligent, but he's from a very rich background, you know?" said Summer, gazing at Alanna curiously. "He is hardly our type, I think he's a bit dull to be honest. His parents own a law firm or something. Didn't you get any money for your birthday?"

Alana ignored the 'dull' comment, putting it down to her sister's inability to appreciate class when she saw it. "Yes, but Dad took all the money off me immediately, for our surfing trip at Christmas; he said I'll need spending money." She blushed, at the sound of how childish that sounded.

"You should ask Dad for some of it back, it's yours after all," Summer suggested simply. "Also, Bethany might want to go; but if I know her, you'll have to pay for the two of you."

Alana tried Bethany first, not yet ready to face her father.

"Cruise around the harbour all day?" Bethany queried, "expenses paid by my lovely sister, surrounded by beautiful people and food and wine? Are you kidding me? Yup, count me in, it's a no brainer!" she grinned, as she leapt out the door, heading to a date with her latest victim.

Her father frowned. "What beach does he surf at? Do I know him?"

"No Dad, he's not a surfer," Alana said hastily. "Well, I don't think he is anyway; but that's okay, and I'm sure he plays some other kind of sport. Besides, not everyone surfs, you know, I mean there are billions of people worldwide who can't even get to a beach."

"Poor sods," he said ruefully, clearly musing on the unimaginable. "Maybe we could start a charity to fund trips to the surf, I don't see how anyone can stay sane without it."

"Yes Dad, great idea, let's talk about that later, but um, well, this yacht they are hiring, I need to chip in for me and Bethany, it's for a whole afternoon on the harbour, you see, lunch and drinks all included, it will only be six hundred dollars for the two of us."

"Six hundred!" her father roared. "For lunch! Why can't you just paddle out to a remote beach on a stand-up board and have a picnic like your mother and I did on our first date?"

"Dad, you met Mum on some deserted island in the middle of nowhere, and I've told you, he's not a surfer."

"Look, if this boy likes you, he should be paying $600 to take YOU out for lunch, not the other way round!"

She decided to skip the speech she had planned about it being her birthday money after all and she could do with it whatever she liked.

Later that day, she had a long surf, pouring all her energies into catching as many waves as she could, until she was exhausted and all thoughts about mysterious, good-looking young men on expensive sailing boats had left her mind. Afterwards, as she was lying on the beach, her board beside her, she began to feel a bit foolish, her father's words echoing in her mind. After all, if Caspian really wanted to get to know her, he just had to ask her sister for her phone number.

She closed her eyes and lay there, basking in the warm afternoon sun. But just as she was just dozing off, a heavy scent of sandalwood and a soft jingle of charms, chased away the freshness of the day. Someone sat down next to her, scudding sharp pinpricks of sand against her face.

Alana was startled and sat up quickly.

A strange woman was sitting next to her. "That's a beautiful board you have there," the woman said in a soft, silky voice.

"I'm sorry, can I help you?" replied Alana, rather stiffly.

"Maybe you can. Or maybe I can help you?" The woman had thick, glossy black hair and a lean, muscular body like a killer shark's, moving in closer. "How much do you want for your board?" she asked intently.

"I'm not sure what you mean," said Alana, pulling her board protectively towards her. It had been her mother's as a young woman, and all the girls had learned on it.

"I'll give you $600 for it. You could do a lot with that money, a pretty girl like you, maybe find the man of your dreams?" the woman smiled, her eyes cold and black.

Alana shivered, and yet a treacherous thought was rising, it was exactly the amount she needed for Caspian's party. "It's not for sale," she faltered.

"That's a Glass Slipper board, with an original signature too. I've been looking for one, for a long time," the woman said coldly. "Here's my card, my shop is in a back-lane near the Corso. Come find me when you change your mind."

Slater arrived at that moment and the woman silently slipped away. He picked up the business card that lay untouched on the sand. "What's this, Vintage Surfboards? You're not selling your board, are you? Wasn't it your mother's? Isn't it the only one you've got, since your new one split in two after that massive dump the other month?"

Alana reflected that having a friend who knew everything about you could be inconvenient at times. "No, of course I'm not selling it," she said irritably and quickly changed the subject.

The following weekend it was perfect sailing weather, as Alana and Bethany packed their bags for the cruise with Caspian and his friends. Alana had the $600 from the sale of the surfboard, hanging around her neck in a small purse. She justified the decision to sell it in a thousand ways, but none of them prevented her heart beating uncomfortably, as they said goodbye to their family. Technically, the board was hers, each of the girls had been given something special of their mother's, but she knew her father would be devastated, when he found out.

"I still can't work out how you can afford this," said Bethany. "But hey, I'm all in. It's going to be an amazing day."

"Thanks Beth, I can't tell you what this means to me!" she said, giving her sister a hug.

Still, the money burned as Alana handed it over to Caspian

and walked across the gangway with Bethany, onto an enormous yacht anchored at the Spit Harbour. The beauty of the yachts, clustered around their awnings and mansions built into cliffs overlooking a smooth blue harbour, could not quite ease the ache in her heart.

The boat was a vast dazzling hulk of white, with smooth lines and untapped power, an open ocean yacht that could handle high seas. A professional skipper and crew were on board, along with two catering staff to look after the twenty or more people who Caspian had invited to come out for the day.

After a brief safety talk by the skipper, with strict instructions to wear lifejackets, which Caspian and some of his friends promptly ignored, they were free to relax and enjoy the ride. As Alana and her sister pulled on their life-jackets, she noticed that there was a beaten-up surfboard tucked away among the life-boats, which she found strangely comforting.

Bethany was soon deep in conversation with a young man, who had sleek black hair, a sharp sense of fashion, and clearly also a sense of humour, as he appeared to be more amused by Bethany than seduced. Alana wondered if Bethany had finally met her match. There was a slightly dazed look on her sister's face, at having to make actual conversation in order to sustain a guy's interest.

Everyone was very friendly, and Alana was soon swept up into the party, enjoying meeting people from a different way of life. But once the initial 'so glad you could come, make yourself at home' from Caspian was over, he barely spoke two words to her. True, he waved at her a few times and made apologetic signs, but unbidden into her mind came images of Slater waving at her to come closer, or moving towards her, no matter who was around.

Still, wasn't she once again in the same room, albeit on a boat, as Caspian? A shy young woman, whom Alana had noticed in Caspian's group at her party, was also there and they were soon instant best friends. It turned out that she was Caspian's sister, although Alana would much rather have been talking to Caspian himself. Once again, an unwelcome thought reminded her that the only time Slater ever left her alone with his brothers was when he was reluctantly forced to go to work.

Another thing was also threatening to mar the day… In the morning, the skies had been a perfect blue, with white clouds slowly scudding across the sky. Now a dark storm front was moving in ominously from the south. A sharp wind stirred up the waves, with tiny sprays of white streaming away from them, in the grey light of the approaching storm.

The skipper decided to head back to shore, reassuring them that it was just a safety precaution as the front was predicted to miss the Northern Beaches. But just as they were starting to relax, the storm swiftly changed direction, attacking them with a suddenness and ferocity that would have frightened even the most seasoned of sailors.

In the rush to get life-jackets on, and help the captain and crew secure the boat, there was much jumbling and shoving on deck. The wind tore into them, whipping up waves that made the boat heave in the great swells. People staggered from side to side, desperately trying to get inside as large waves crashed onto the deck.

"Man overboard!" someone screamed suddenly.

"Man overboard!" crew members echoed around the boat, passing it on.

Somehow Alana just knew it was Caspian, and a lifetime of surf-life training kicked in. She saw the crew, going through the drill of spotting a man overboard, with one crew member pointing continuously at Caspian in the water. They scrambled to turn the boat around, but Caspian only had minutes at most. As if in slow motion, she checked her lifejacket, grabbed the surfboard she had seen on deck earlier and, without hesitation, dived into the heaving waves.

The icy cold waters sent shock waves through her system.

"Caspian! Caspian!" she shouted, trying to get a bearing on where he was. Finally she spotted him, waving frantically in the inky black waves.

"Help! I'm here!" he yelled desperately.

She hauled herself onto her board and paddled with all her strength, relieved that he was still shouting. A drowning person is always silent, their body shutting down all other functions to focus on just breathing, on keeping their face above water.

The current was powerful and it pushed against her, again and again. She reached him just as he was going under, and desperately pulled him up to the surface. Together, somehow, they managed to get him onto the board.

But she was not quick enough. Just as she was repositioning Caspian on the surfboard, so she could climb on behind him and paddle them back to safety, an enormous wave roared up, like a black heaving monster of the night. In a wild fury, it dumped all its strength and power upon them. Alana was forced under the water, her hands ripped away from Caspian and the surfboard. She clutched blindly in the water for them, a huge vortex of current pulling her away. The yacht quickly receded, her lifejacket useless amid the relentless waves. Each time she pushed to the surface, gasping to take a breath, water swamped her, pushing her back down again, until she grew desperate for air, coughing and choking on the salty water rushing into her mouth.

With all her energy spent, she felt herself sinking deeper and deeper, into a dark green world, one that was like a second home to her: the sea. Time slowed right down. The air in her lungs faded away and the pressure to just breathe, became unbearable. She thought of all the things she would never do, of her family – who loved her so much – she could not believe this was how her life would end.

Just as she was about to surrender and let the water enter her empty lungs, there in the unknown depths she saw a gentle light. Within that light, beckoning to her, with arms reaching out towards her, was the smiling glowing form of her mother.

'Mum!' she silently screamed, desperately trying to swim towards her.

But her mother stayed out of reach, encouraging her forward.

And then suddenly around Alana were beautiful creatures of the sea, wonderful mermaids, dazzling sea horses and silvery dolphins, all rushing around her. They seemed to support her gently, breathing life into her, just as it was fading away.

Then there was just blackness.

Alana later found out that the crew members had rescued Caspian in a dingy, soon after she had been swept away; but then had been unable to locate her. A helicopter rescue team had found her the next morning, lying on a small beach in the harbour, unconscious but somehow still alive. No one could explain how she had ended up there or how she had survived.

For weeks she had been in intensive care. There had been a possibility of brain damage, and so she had been put into an induced coma, tubes down her throat, unable to speak, unable to walk. Eventually, they had eased her off the sedation. Even then she had been unable to speak. It was as if she was still in that dark green world beneath the sea, with her mother and the mermaids.

At first Caspian had visited her every day, gazing at her with admiration in his eyes, or so the nurses had said. He had talked to them of this fierce young woman who had almost lost her life to save his, and how he longed to hear her voice again.

But, as the days passed, his visits had became fewer and he had returned to his studies, the long vigil had not been for him.

When she finally awoke, the loving faces and familiar voices beside her bed were those of her father and Slater. Her father was reduced now to a shadow of his former self, with his head in his hands; and Slater, sitting beside him, looked just as grim.

"Dad?" Alana managed to whisper.

Her father's mane of hair flew back off his face as he leapt to his feet. "Alana! Thank God, you're back!"

"Where have I been, what's happened?"

Her sisters rushed into the room, her family's energy and love instantly enfolding her.

Slater just sat smiling at her, not his usual boyish grin, but one with suffering now behind it.

∽⌇∾

A few days later, when she awoke from an afternoon rest, Alana noticed something in the room. "What's that over there?" Alana said softly, her voice still not quite her own, as she pointed to a draped blanket in the corner. "That looks suspiciously like a surfboard. Slater, why bother bringing it in here, I can hardly walk, let alone surf!" she smiled weakly at him.

"Yeah, well, maybe it's surfing you should be trying first?" he said casually. "Look, it took me a while to track her down, and I had to work two jobs all summer to pay for it, but I thought this might help, you know, get you back on those waves again. I've missed you out there!" And then, bursting with pride, he handed her the most precious thing in the world, her mother's surfboard.

Inspiration: The Little Mermaid

Alana belongs to a big surfing family with a widowed father, just like the original little mermaid who had three sisters and a father who was widowed. In the original, the little mermaid gives up things which are key to her identity, her voice and her mermaid's tail – Alana gives up her mother's surfboard, something which represents her love of her mother and her skill as a surfer, both of which are also part of her identity. They each give up these things for a young man they have fallen in love with, who is from a different sphere of life. Both save the life of the young man they love when he falls off a boat. Both at some point in their story are unable to speak or walk. In Alana's case, however, it is her best friend who discovers how much she means to him when she nearly drowns, and who makes sacrifices to reclaim her mother's surfboard, knowing it holds the key to her recovery. In the little mermaid, the prince makes no sacrifices. In both stories the 'prince' character is weak. This retelling tries to show, differently to the little mermaid, that no man is worth giving up things that form part of your identity, and that someone who loves you will make sacrifices too, and not expect you to make them all.

Author: Joanna Mawson-Lee

Joanna Mawson-Lee writes novels with spiritual themes, as well as children's stories about magical creatures. She lives in Sydney and works as a freelance policy and procedure writer. She studied English & Philosophy at Swansea University in Wales, UK, and this led to a life-long passion for philosophical literature. In her spare time, she enjoys meditation, walking on the beach and playing beach volleyball. After helping her late husband live successfully with Motor Neurone Disease for several years, she is now focused on helping others through her writing by drawing on her rich life experiences.

Away with the Fairies

Susan Steggall

Nadine had been dreading the day when she would have to clear out her parents' house. Now that day had arrived. She walked slowly up the weed-infested path and opened the front door. Inside, all was still, expectant, as if the house had been waiting for her. Her footsteps echoed on the polished floorboards in the hallway as she made her way to the lounge room. Familiar yet not familiar after an absence of so many years, the sight of sagging armchairs, faded chintz curtains and her mother's treasured Persian rug engulfed her in memories of her long-dead twin sister, Kitty, and shadowy traces of a troubling incident that had darkened Nadine's childhood. She had buried the unhappiness in the deepest corners of her psyche, almost forgotten in a life filled with achievements and adventures. Lovers had come and gone but Nadine never could commit her heart to any of them; there was always a part of her missing.

For the first time in years, Nadine wanted to see Kitty's face. She took the family photograph album from the bookshelf, sat down and opened it. The earliest photographs were of her parents' wedding and their new house. Next were photos of Nadine and Kitty. As babies they had been very alike – the same round faces and turned-up noses, the same curly chestnut hair. The only way to tell them apart was that Nadine had green eyes and Kitty's were hazel.

After their third birthday, differences began to appear. Nadine was strong and sturdy while Kitty grew paler and thinner, content to sit and watch her more energetic twin. By the time they were four it was clear Kitty was ailing. Their parents took her to doctor after doctor but none of them could find what was wrong. In the last photo of Kitty, the girl was little more than a wraith in their mother's arms. Nadine could hear their mother's sad voice as if it were yesterday.

"Kitty was very ill and could not get better. Like all children who die young, she went away to the Country of the Fairies and we never saw her again."

Nadine missed her sister badly. "I wish I'd gone too," she often said.

"And leave me and Father?" her mother would whisper.

"I would only go for a little while to see Kitty in the Country of the Fairies, just like we visit Aunt Louise at Christmas time. But I don't know where the fairies live."

Her father would chime in. "Animals are supposed to talk to the fairies. They might know."

Nadine thought for a moment, then nodded. "I'll stay, for now. One day when I'm older I'll search for Kitty."

"Let's go to the park," her mother would say, a catch in her throat.

At the delightful prospect of swings and slippery-dip Nadine took her parents' hands and skipped away from the sadness of losing her sister...

Nadine used to know the names of all the trees in the park and wondered how many she would remember after so many years. She closed the album, grabbed a coat against the late-June chill and headed to the gardens, a place where her childhood imagination had once roamed free. Nadine smiled as she walked across lawns sprinkled with the last of autumn's fallen leaves, their flecks of gold merging with the dappled light filtering through the foliage of eucalypts, date palms and a solitary bottle tree. She approached the sandstone ledges that rose in tiers towards the escarpment on the park's western boundary and sat on a wide slab of rock. She ran her hands over its sand-papery surface, sniffed appreciatively at the faint resinous odour of a nearby radiata pine. A golden butterfly fluttered past on its way to a clump of native clematis near a smooth-barked angophora. A rainbow lorikeet called imperiously to its mate. Nadine closed her eyes…

⌁❧⌁

"Hello Nadine, it's me, Kitty," a child's voice called. "I am so happy to see you again. Do you want to visit my home in Fairy Country?" At Nadine's enthusiastic nod, Kitty continued. "Because we are so alike, I can transform you into a pretend fairy, but you must promise never to try and approach me. If you do the fairies will know you are not me, only a human being, and terrible things will happen. If a human is admitted into Fairy Country there will be a great disaster."

Nadine was enthralled at the prospect of visiting the Fairy Country, but more than that she was eager to see her sister again; she would agree to Kitty's terms, for the moment. "How do I find this magical country?" she asked excitedly.

"The animals will guide you," Kitty replied, her voice growing fainter until it faded altogether.

When Nadine judged it safe to look, she discovered that the park stretched further than the eye could see. The trees were truly enormous. The flowers on a nearby banksia were like the bristling yellow cylinders at a carwash. The rock on which she sat had become a vast platform; the ground was now far below. She was no bigger than a willy wagtail.

Instead of jeans and sweater, she was wearing a pink organza dress — identical to one she had worn as a child. Her brown leather shoes had been transformed into strange silver slippers with wing-like protrusions. She put a hand to her hair. Instead of her smooth chignon, she felt the unruly curls of childhood. Was she dreaming? She didn't think so. The stone on which she sat was rough against her skin, the sun warm on her face. A thrill of fear ran through her.

She heard a rustling under some nearby ferns and turned to see a grey-brown bandicoot emerge. "Who are you?" the animal asked.

"I could ask the same of you," Nadine replied, surprised at her childish voice, so unlike her adult one. "My name is Nadine and I want to visit the Country of the Fairies, to see where Kitty lives. Can you help me?"

The bandicoot eyed Nadine with bright black eyes. "Why it's here, all around you, if you know how to look. First you will have to get off that cliff. Try jumping."

"It's a long way down," Nadine said, wriggling to the edge of the rock and peering over, her heart beating fast.

"You'll just have to trust yourself," the bandicoot replied and scurried off.

Nadine took a deep breath and pushed herself forward. To her surprise she didn't flop to the ground but floated, light as dandelion down, into a thick layer of leaves, some as big as dinner plates.

As Nadine stood up, a throaty voice called out: "You did that all right." A huge lizard with blue flashes on its head and tail waddled into view.

"Aha," Nadine said when the lizard flicked out its tongue at a passing fly. "You're a blue-tongue!"

"How did you guess?"

"Where am I?" Nadine ignored his ironic tone.

"The Land of Minnows," the lizard chortled. "Most people here are tiny, like you; not me. I'm full size. All the better to catch my dinner." He trapped two more hapless flies, swallowed them in one gulp then wiped his mouth with a scaly claw. "Delicious!"

Nadine was glad she didn't have proper wings. No flying creature would be safe from those jaws. "I'm looking for the Country of the Fairies," she said. "Perhaps you could show me the way."

The lizard's head swayed from side to side. "Could do," he said, "but you'll have to cross the river first."

In the 'real world' the stream that meandered through the park was usually little more than a trickle, and easily crossed. However it had been raining and in her current Lilliputian state, Nadine acknowledged that traversing it might pose a problem.

"Thank you, lizard. Can you show me the way?"

"Call me Bluey. Come on."

She followed him across rocks and around bushes and was clambering through a clump of bright green cycads when she heard a sound like small bells tinkling. Looking up she saw dozens of fairy-like creatures dressed in rainbow colours, rising into the sky on shimmering wings. Her heart leapt. Was Kitty among them? The fairy flock was so high she could not see their faces. She tried to follow but they were travelling very fast. Even with her winged feet, she made slow progress and could only watch as they vanished; the lizard also disappeared.

She sank into a tuft of spongy moss under the graceful branches of a weeping lilly-pilly. She felt like weeping herself. In this strange land, was there no one to help her find Kitty? Water sparkled in the distance, but the way to it appeared difficult, across huge tree roots that fanned out in all directions. With a sigh she struggled onwards and finally reached the swiftly flowing stream. It was much wider than she had imagined it to be, with no obvious way to cross it. If she abandoned her quest, she had no idea how to get back to her proper life. She might be stuck here – wherever 'here' was – forever.

At the sound of a melodious tune, Nadine glanced up to see a young butcherbird sitting on a low-hanging branch. Although the bird had a sharply hooked beak it seemed friendly.

"Hello," Nadine said.

The fledgling began singing a song about 'Poor little Kitty'. Nadine felt a moment of anxiety. If her companion assumed she was Kitty then every other creature she met might make the same mistake.

"I'm on my way to sing for the Fairy Queen – that's why I'm

practising. I'm surprised you are not already there, Kitty," the bird trilled, eyeing Nadine with suspicion. "Perhaps you are afraid to cross the dreaded Spi-Woman's river. I'm not good at flying yet, so Mother won't let me go over the river by myself in case the Spi-Woman pulls me down into her cavern."

As a make-believe fairy Nadine could skim just above the ground, but she couldn't fly high like birds and genuine fairies so she too would be in danger. "Is there a way round?"

"No, the river goes all the way to the sea. No one knows where it begins."

The bird stretched both wings as its mother arrived and the two flew off.

Nadine dipped a toe in the cold water. There was a ripple close by as a strange object began to break the surface to reveal the weirdest looking creature Nadine had ever seen: a woman covered in green-grey scales from the top of her head to her fish-like tail. Her hair was coarse and crinkly like seaweed and her fingers had claws instead of nails.

"You want to get across my river, dearie?" she gurgled. "Come along, I'll take you."

"Do you live here?" Nadine asked to buy time, hoping the butcherbird had exaggerated the danger.

"I have a lovely house down under the water. It's made of precious crystal. Would you like to see it?"

"Why do you need a house?"

"I must live in the water but be surrounded by air; to breathe, you see."

Nadine didn't really 'see' but nodded all the same.

"Spirit People like me keep the ponds cleaned out and rivers and streams free from rubbish so their water flows freely to the sea. Otherwise the waterways would choke up, the levels rise, spread over the whole country and drown all those who live there."

The Spi-Woman waved her claws. "The way humans are behaving, a great flood is inevitable. The seas and oceans are rising, in spite of our best efforts." Her voice came in angry staccato bursts.

Nadine resolved to try harder when she was back in her own world to keep the beaches clean. She brushed aside a small voice that said, '*if* you get back'.

She was about to let the Spi-Woman ferry her across when a wren flew by, twittering, "Don't go". Before Nadine could ask why, the bird was gone in a flash of blue.

"It won't take long, will it?" she asked.

"Not at all," replied the Spi-Woman, a leering grin on her face, a wicked gleam in her eyes.

Nadine was about to say 'yes' she would like to be ferried across, when the wren darted past again and chirped, louder this time, "Don't go!"

As Nadine backed away from the edge of the river, the Spi-Woman began to sink slowly under the surface. At that moment a dragonfly swooped near Nadine, its wings beating fast. In an instant she leapt onto the shining armour behind its head. But the dragonfly did not ferry Nadine straight across the water. He swooped high and low in great curves with a whole cloud of dragonflies chasing them in a game of follow-the-leader. Finally, when the dragonfly flew close enough to the opposite side of the river, Nadine jumped onto the shore.

She leant over the side hoping to catch a glimpse of the Spi-Woman's crystal house, only to find the creature looking straight up at her, waving her long scaly arms round and round in circles. The water in the river began to swirl in eddies, faster and faster. Its level rose until it lapped over the banks. Just as the Spi-Woman's snaky arms reached out towards her, Nadine somersaulted backwards and landed on the velvety petals of a flannel flower. She sat up and looked around. If this was Fairy Country where was the Queen, and all the fairies?

Suddenly voices tinkled ahead of her, chanting in unison: "Where is Kitty? We must keep looking for her."

Nadine followed the voices, leaping over ferns and creepers until she reached the spreading roots of a Port Jackson fig tree. In her haste she tripped and sprawled head first in the damp soil. "Bother," she cried.

A band of fairies crowded around her calling: "Here's Kitty, dear Kitty. Where have you been?"

Before Nadine could answer, the fairies gathered her up and hurried to a hillock on which more fairies danced and sang about their duties for the Fairy Queen: one was to guide the tendrils on the plants; another to gather dead blooms and bury them in the soil; a third was to waken seeds from their winter sleep. Nadine tried to make herself invisible behind a spreading fern. Since the fairies assumed she was Kitty, it would soon be her turn. If she didn't contribute something they might all notice her eyes were green, instead of Kitty's hazel.

"Kitty, Kitty," the fairies chorused. "Kitty hasn't sung yet. We all know what she does!"

Into Nadine's head came a rhyme from childhood, about waiting on the Fairy Queen 'in her lovely robe of spangled green'. But she couldn't sing it and stood there becoming redder and redder, as they all stared at her.

"Why Kitty," asked one fairy, "where is the Queen and why aren't you with her?"

A tall fairy asked why Nadine didn't sing.

Another stared at her closely and said she looked different.

A fourth asked, "What have you done to your eyes?"

Just then the music changed to a loud clangour of bells, which distracted the fairies and gave Nadine time to escape.

She skimmed around tree trunks and over the undergrowth to reach a slope covered with emerald grass and rimmed by bangalay gums and carabeen trees. About half way down the sward, a vine of pink boronia grew so thickly over a fallen tree it formed a kind of grotto. Nadine tiptoed towards it and, as she got closer she saw, sticking out from under the mass of blooms, a small bare foot. Nadine brushed aside her sister's warning that something awful would happen if they met face-to-face and peeped into the bower to find a heap of lustrous pale-green fabric. As Nadine bent down to lift the flowers, from behind her peals of mischievous laughter erupted. The fairies had followed her!

The green-clad figure in the bower stirred, sat up and reached for a stem of boronia bush, which she then held upright, like a wand. It was the Fairy Queen. Nadine was so astonished that she forgot everything she ought to have remembered and shouted, "You're not Kitty!"

There was a crackling of twigs as she spoke and through the boronia screen a figure, who had been lying on the other side of the Fairy Queen, sprang up and dashed away. She did not see the face but even through the leaves she recognised a pink dress identical to her own and knew it was Kitty.

As the Queen inspected Nadine from head to toe, a lightning flash shot into the royal fairy's eyes. Suddenly there arose a mighty gust of wind; the sky turned black and darkness fell around them. A terrible storm blew up, the wind and rain howling like demons. Nadine crouched down and covered her face with her hands.

As suddenly as it had begun the wind stopped. Nadine raised her head to find she was alone: fairies, Fairy Queen and floral bower had vanished. Yet it was the same grassy slope with the same trees growing around it; next to her was a stem of boronia, crushed and torn. This must be the 'great disaster' Kitty had told her about, and it was Nadine's disobedience that had caused it. If she could have her time over again, she would be content simply to visit the country where Kitty lived, and not try to see her sister face to face. But somewhere, in a different time and place, Nadine knew she had ruined any possibility of another chance.

A rumbling sound made Nadine look up to see a bizarre figure on the edge of the slope. She hurried towards it to find a tall old man wrapped in a long brown cloak, his head so bowed he was nearly bent double. Before she got close enough to ask what had happened to the Fairy Queen, the old man was swept into the last of the storm and disappeared up and over the escarpment at the back of the park; it was as if nothing had happened.

Desperate to find out, Nadine set off through the park in search of someone to ask. Near the trunk of an immense eucalypt, she came upon two koalas sitting side by side on a pile of leaves. They stared at her solemnly.

"Did you notice a storm just now?" Nadine asked.

The bigger koala wagged his furry head, which she understood to mean 'yes'.

"Do you often have storms like that?" she continued.

"Only once in a while," said the smaller koala.

"What do you mean by 'once in a while'? Have you ever had one in the past?"

"Not in the past… in a while I said."

"Do you think something has happened to the Fairy Queen?"

The koalas waved their paws. "That's it – the Fairy Queen. She's gone!"

"Where has she gone?"

"Only the Tree-Man knows."

"Where shall I find the Tree-Man?"

The koalas cuddled closer.

"I must find him and ask him to release the Queen," said Nadine. "It's all my fault." The koalas looked dismal; Nadine's heart sank.

"I must find him," she insisted. "It's because of me it all happened. Please tell me where I can find the Tree-Man."

"In the middle of the park." The larger koala pointed to a sombre gully.

"Will you show me the way?"

When the Koalas didn't reply, Nadine continued. "Will the Tree-Man hurt you?"

"No, but we are animals."

"Why are you afraid then?"

"You are a fairy person."

"You think he'll harm me?"

The koalas nodded but agreed to accompany her.

The trio had not gone far into a dark glade filled with tree ferns and grass trees before they met a pelican waddling along a path.

Nadine waved to the bird. "Can you tell us what has happened?"

"A Great Disaster, Kitty," the pelican replied.

"Is it the Fairy Queen?"

"She has been carried away." The pelican clacked its beak.

"How can I discover where the Fairy Queen has gone?"

"Only the Tree-Man can tell you that."

Then the pelican muttered: "That's strange; that's very strange." With a great flapping of wings, he launched himself into the air.

At each new creature Nadine encountered, the answer to her questions met with the same responses: "A Great Disaster" or "That's strange, that's very strange." Always, only the Tree-Man could help her. Two platypuses, a dwarf tree frog, a bush rat, a kookaburra and several magpies all said the same thing: "It was strange – very strange."

As she approached the darkest part of the park, Nadine sensed an important moment was near. She didn't want to show the animals following her that she was afraid yet when they came to a clearing, she gripped the koalas' paws tightly. At first she saw only the stump of a huge Port Jackson fig, flanked by the ringed trunks of tall palm-trees. When she looked more closely she saw it was the Tree-Man himself. He had two withered branch-like arms and a gnarled face halfway up the leathery trunk. He looked very like the old gardener at her parents' home. Nadine felt a shiver of fear. The gardener used to stare at her in a funny way and she'd always made sure never to be alone with him.

The Tree-Man spoke: "So you've come. I knew you would."

Nadine said nothing but she could tell by the look in his eye that he knew she was not Kitty, only a human girl pretending to be a fairy.

"Well, what did you come for?"

The animals were listening eagerly, and she wanted to appear brave even though she was quaking inside. "I came to find out what has happened to the Fairy Queen," she replied, hoping the Tree-Man wouldn't notice her shaky voice.

"You were there, you know what happened," he replied sternly.

"I saw a great storm, and an old, old man…"

The Tree-Man laughed so hard his branches shook. "I am very old, even for a tree. Hundreds of years old. So when I choose to be a man for a little while, I am of a very great age. That is beside the point. What I mean is that you know why what happened – happened."

She could have said 'I don't know what you mean,' but she did know what he meant and could not answer; she jiggled from one foot to the other.

"I'll tell you then," the Tree-Man said. "In the good old days,

I was King of the park. Then the fairies came and we trees fought and fought. They were stronger than us, with their nasty magic. We had magic too, although it wasn't as good as theirs. Still we could make it unpleasant for them. In the end we made a treaty. Do you know what a treaty is?"

Before Nadine could say, 'yes like the Treaty of Versailles, after World War I', the Tree-Man continued.

"It often means the weaker side gives up almost everything to be allowed to keep something important. In this case the treaty was that we should remain trees all the time, and not go running about where we liked and turning into humans when we chose, as we had been in the habit of doing. We were to be trees, rooted to the soil, except – this was our side of it – except if the fairies ever allowed a human being to enter the country.

"We didn't want people here, with their axes and loppings and cuttings, as once we were real trees we didn't feel safe unless the fairies promised us that. So they agreed that if ever a human entered their country, we should be free once more to take human shape as we used to do and exercise our power over the weather."

He nodded, stiffly. "Oh yes, trees have power over the weather. When word got out that a human being had entered this wood, I crashed out, free again. My brave companions are all dead and these trees," he waved his craggy arms, "are Johnny-come-latelies. I alone can be alive. I have shown these fairies what I can do."

By the time he had finished this long speech the animals were craning their necks to stare at Nadine, their voices bouncing off one another.

"I knew it wasn't Kitty."

"There's something strange about her."

"Kitty's got hazel eyes. Didn't I say so?"

"Whoever heard of a fairy with green eyes?"

"Then it isn't Kitty."

"Could Kitty change her eyes?"

Nadine put her hands over her ears to shut out this chatter. She turned to the Tree-Man. "It was you who carried off the Fairy Queen and it all happened because of me. I am so sorry. Can't you let her go?"

"Ha-ha," laughed the Tree-Man. "What would become of Kitty then? Wouldn't the Fairy Queen be very angry with Kitty for letting you in and giving control back to the trees?"

"I think she would forgive her because, you see, I am Kitty's twin sister and she did it because I wanted to see her very much. I'm sure the Fairy Queen will forgive Kitty, if you'll let her go. Oh please do! I'll do anything you ask, if you'll only let her go."

"Anything, will you?" asked the Tree-Man grimly. "Do you know I eat human beings, plump and tender like you? Will you come and be eaten up?"

Nadine wasn't sure if he was joking or not. He really did resemble that old gardener and she didn't like it one bit. The memory of the bowed old man on the grassy slope bothered her too. Suppose she crawled inside the Tree-Man and found that old man there? For a split second, Nadine felt a flash of terror as she remembered her parents' garden shed and her young self, struggling to break free of strong soil-stained hands. She trembled as she asked, "What must I do?"

"You would have to crawl into that large crack down there between my roots," he answered.

"I don't think I'll fit."

"Then you'll leave the Fairy Queen to her fate, whatever that may be." He cackled horribly. Nadine knew she must forget the past if she were to save the Fairy Queen. She dashed forward before she had time to be afraid. On her hands and knees she crawled into the yawning blackness at the foot of the tree stump. The animals gave loud cries of fear; the koalas groaned a deep 'woo-oof'. The instant she was inside the darkness, a loud explosion rent the air and the tree flew to pieces all round her. She seemed to be floating high up in the sky. She saw the animals scattering in all directions as bits of wood rained down on them. As she rose higher still, she saw a velvety green hillock. On its top stood the Fairy Queen with her hair falling like waves of sunshine over her shoulders. As Nadine watched, Kitty came running up. The Fairy Queen held out her arms and Kitty ran straight into them. Then Kitty and the Fairy Queen disappeared in the mist that had begun to swirl through the park.

There was a flash of lightening, a crack of thunder, and the sound of wood tearing as the top of a massive hoop pine came crashing down on Nadine, pinning her legs to the ground. She felt an intense pain in her side and moved her arm to locate its source. Her hand came away covered in blood. She screamed for help, but no one came. She lost all sense of time. Sometimes she was in great pain, at other times she couldn't feel anything at all. As she drifted in and out of consciousness, as her life ebbed away, soothing images of Kitty in the Country of the Fairies flowed past Nadine's eyes. She didn't want to wake up, but stay with her sister, and never again be troubled by human wrongdoings.

Nadine heard Kitty whisper, "Nadine, Nadine" amidst the bell-like voices of the fairies.

"I'm coming, Kitty," she called ever so faintly.

Inspiration: The Little Fairy Sister

Based on 'The Little Fairy Sister' by Ida Rentoul Outhwaite & Grenbry Outhwaite, A & C Black, Ltd, London (first printed, 1923, reprinted 1929).

Bridget, an 8-year-old girl whose twin sister died when they were very young, longs to see her sister again; and one afternoon, while drowsing in a hammock, she is transported to the Country of the Fairies where she is greeted by her sister, Nancy, who turns her into a make-believe fairy – on the condition that Bridget does not try to approach Nancy. Otherwise something terrible will happen.

In the Country of the Fairies, curiosity gets the better of Bridget. She tries to meet her sister, with dire consequences, the moral being: 'disobey the gods (here read fairies) and they will punish you'. In the original story there is a happy ending.

My version, transposed to contemporary times with Nadine and Kitty, is darker.

Northern Beaches Writers' Group

Author: Susan Steggall

Susan Steggall's publications include 'Alpine Beach: A Family Adventure', novels 'Forget Me Not', 'It Happened Tomorrow' and ''Tis the Doing not the Deed', plus art-related articles, book and exhibition reviews, book chapters and essays. 'A Most Generous Scholar: Joan Kerr, Art and Architectural Historian' was a non-fiction winner in the 2013 SWW's Biennial Book Awards. Her story 'A Poetical Science' appeared in 'A Fearsome Engine' (Zena Shapter ed, Northern Beaches Writers' Group, 2016). Susan has edited anthologies for the Society of Women Writers and was editor of the ISAA Review (the journal of the Independent Scholars Association of Australia Inc) from 2010 to 2015. Her story 'Ebb and Flow at the Margins' was published in 'Saltwater', celebrating community creativity with stories, poetry and art (Zena Shapter ed, Northern Beaches Council, 2019).

Snoring Ugly

Mijmark

A long time ago (remember the Howard years? We'd thought we'd forgotten about them too) in a galax... an outback far, far away... okay, the western-Sydney suburb (close enough) of Funnydunnydo – out there, there was a cause for alarm. The ground rumbled. The traffic jumbled. The people stumbled. The rugby team fumbled. The council mumbled. Everyone felt bothered yet also very humbled. Why? She snored like nothing else, and grew wriggling brown snakes from her piebald scalp – they simply petrified mummy into a heart attack. Little Orphan Awful learnt to terrorise the town. Oh what fun!

She crashed birthday parties. She crashed wedding receptions. She crashed school fetes. She crashed cars when she crossed the street, the owners swerving to avoid even looking at her.

She out-hooned the goons on the streets who tried ganging up on her, earning her the tag-line 'Mad-Ussa', instead of Madame Ussa, as she petrified them with fear. The council at least enjoyed the very life-like statues that they used to decorate their city parks. Others hurled abuse and foul language at her from afar, which she seemed to feed upon, growing bigger and more hideous by the day.

Council eventually passed a law banning her. However, police avoided her after too many crashed squad cars and loss of officers, who ended up as decorations to their now crowded statue gardens in city parks. Bullets even swerved away when fired, too scared to venture anywhere near her.

Mad-Ussa reigned supreme. Those snake-hairs did like to eat their Gorgon-zola cakes from the Cheesecake Shop, her local hangout.

The council had to seek out desperate measures. They hunted down the wisdom of the old ways and soon asked for advice from the local Indigenous Land Council. That mob brought in an elder whose insight was renowned. Auntie told them, "You must put her to sleep and send her away, somewhere in an impenetrable bubble where she wouldn't cause anyone further harm."

The mayor then decided, "We'll send her to Canberra!"

They arranged for a mighty corroboree; it was to be that night around the crumbled ruins of the bankrupt Cheesecake Shop. They danced with fervour the chant of the long sleep, weaving into their magic a slumbering curse, where only pursed lips from a froggy Prince fan could wake her. It was a gambol, but they pulled it off with twinkling toes, lots of mellow bellows and purple raindrops sprinkled upon her wrinkled hide.

But she still snored abhorrently! Doctors tried C-pap machines, yet she ate the contraptions in her slumber – burp! Removalists buckled under the strain of shifting her; their wobbling legs barely lifting her bulk. Trucks taking her on her queen-sized bedlam constantly broke down, shaken apart by her rumbling slumbering, like a spammer thrown into the works.

They asked the people of Yass for help, but they said 'no'. The leaders of Collector wouldn't collect her. The mayor of Franklin frankly denied all requests. She demoralised the people of Downer, what a downer! Their endeavour seemed doomed, until the Queen Bee of Queanbeyan sweetened the deal with shipments of honey. No politician could resist such saccharin praise from news-media's ways.

So, Mad-Ussa arrived, entombed in the bubble, buried deeply beneath Parliament House, and all were safe... for a while. But who knew? Radioactive zombies – abhorred by Senator Lambie – were still running the place. Such a disgrace! Sonorous snoring was sweet music to their ears, so they secretly sought her out to replace him.

Years later, global warming brought cane toads into Lake Burley Griffin. Sure enough, they were all Prince fans, even wearing raspberry berets every other day. Mad-Ussa's hazardous minions of carbon-14 emissions cooked up a plot – coal-fired of course. These atomic, glowing goons of fallout lured one brave amphibian aboard to embrace their quest. Paul E Wog of the One Notion Party followed the radiation trail to her tomb using a guy/girl counter, a statistical device left over by the last census debacle. They would be done with Senator Lambie!

Deafened by her ruckus, this warty toad ventured deep down into her abode, intending to uncover complex, covert conspiracies covered up in a steamy swamp of secrets – a perfect place for his kind. But beauty being in the eye of this beholder, he soon swooned by her side and gave himself the kiss of death upon sleazy, slimy lips, waking her – at which point he croaked. She enjoyed the frog-leg breakfast – burp.

But having imbibed his toxic-skinned rhetoric, Mad-Ussa awoke from below with an evil purpose, to Aussify all immigrants into ocker, tinny-wielding, ossified statues wearing Akubras – mate!

With toad-worthy insight, she arose from below. With a vicious vengeance she landed her blows. With her radioactive zombies to faction the party, she then ran for office, a public display to everyone's dismay. Her snoring literally shook the place up. Audiences watching her speak soon succumbed as well, stoned into submission at the mere sight of her serpentine hairstyle.

She was so horrible, so caustic, so callous, so vicious that naturally everyone voted for her and her petty, pretty policies of cheesecake for all. And that's how Mad-Ussa became Prime Minister to live happily ever after... until she died of a fatal heart attack from hardened arteries – all that cholesterol of her cheesecake only diet.

So that, my friends, is why we let sleeping dogs lie – about everything, in politics.

Inspiration: Sleeping Beauty

'Snoring Ugly' is based loosely – quite loosely – upon 'Sleeping Beauty'. However, there are allusions to other tales and myths, like 'The Frog-Prince' and the Greek/Roman gorgon Medusa, just for twists and turns to thicken the plot, like one thickens gravy into a gloopy mess.

Of Beasts & Butterflies

Author: Mijmark

Mijmark (mïj'-mark): n, adj. Its origins are random. The word came to describe a quality of a contradiction of terms that transmuted from imagination to reality.

1) It's not just a pseudonym for an author of subversive literature who embraces this concept whole-heartedly, for its subsequent meaning cannot truly be defined; its definition must be subtly to radically different from one person to another. Its emphasis describes the polarizations between designations found between individuals, how one person views green and another chartreuse, or jade, or verdant, or olive, etc... Therefore the word must possess an individual, gestalt definition.

Whatever that means, it's up to you, and that's the point.

2) Sometimes Mijical.

Sorcerer's Apprentice

Suzi Green

Kick-ass, high-flying, apprentice-CEO, that's how they describe me at Packaging Please. What they should call me is Amelia-who-Ameliorates, because when I travel to the farthest flung parts of Australia to do business improvement I make everything faster and more efficient. When the boss suggested I visit the Toogelooga outback branch, 400kms south of Alice Springs, my mission was to kick things up and reduce head count. I love how many ways there are to say, 'fire your ass', nicely; and each time I went somewhere new I tried to think up a new one to use. This time, however, I first had to kick around a lot of red dust.

It started with a flight from Sydney to Alice on a Sunday night, then a long drive the next morning to the land of droughts. I arrived in Toogelooga looking like I'd been to a Hindu Holi Festival of Colour where they had run out of everything except ochre. How was I ever going to stay clean?

Since it was too early to check into the hotel, I skipped lunch and made my way straight to the plant where Packaging Please housed its 28-person team. By way of a pep talk I sang in the car, in the style of Italian opera, a song about a beautiful Amelia: 'Amelia, mia bella, amore'. It always enhanced my inner mojo prior to ripping a dysfunctional team into shreds. I was still singing at top voice when I rounded the corner into the industrial estate, and nearly ran over two people lolloping across the road. As I swallowed my final words of self-love, I mouthed an apologetic 'sorry', then went back to concentrating on the printout showing me where I needed to go.

There was one huge building on an unnecessarily large ten-acre site. Land was cheap in the middle of nowhere. I parked by the main employee entrance, but after standing in the sun outside the locked door for several minutes, I wondered if it was a public holiday. Perhaps it was an outback thing? I'd never been to any of our regional sites, despite having worked for the company for thirteen years – since I graduated, in fact. How time flies when you're scaling your way up the corporate skyscraper.

Still not seeing anyone and with no obvious route inside, I made my way around the outside of the building, hugging the shade. Where the overhang widened, an Indigenous woman was sitting on the ground weaving a large mat. I was mesmerised by her hands, magically pulling and threading. I gave her a wide berth, not wanting to disturb her ritual, even though it meant venturing into the glare of the sun.

I eventually found the delivery entrance where there was a hive of activity; well, as much as anyone could expect in a place where it was 30 degrees mid-winter. I smiled, expecting a grand greeting. I got a couple of nods from people in blue overalls as they fled into the bowels of the warehouse. One man came toward me.

"I'm looking for..." I rummaged through my tote for the introduction page provided by my boss.

"You'll be wanting Martha," said a short guy with a leathery face. "She's having a smoko. She'll be back in a minute. Why don't you take a seat over there?" He pointed to some metal chairs in the corner.

"Thank you. I'm..." I wanted to introduce myself, but suddenly the outback dust got stuck in my throat and I broke into a huge coughing fit. I made it to the closest chair.

The guy suppressed a smirk and walked over to a cupboard above a sink, where he rifled through a selection of mismatched mugs. I made a mental note to order some branded drinkware for the site, wondering if these places got left behind when corporate enhancements were taking place. After a quick rinse, he filled a vessel with water from the tap and bought it back to me. He watched while I gulped down the refreshing liquid, then collected the mug from me, gave it a wipe with a tea towel and put it back in the cupboard.

"Thank you. I..." I stood to shake his hand, but the long strap on my bag caught under my chair and somehow wrapped itself around my ankle. I stumbled forward, pulling the bag and chair with my leg. Struggling to keep myself upright, I took one step, then a second. My double hop saved me from doing a complete face plant, but my dignity was a little fragile.

My new friend seemed to avoid eye contact. "There she is, coming back now." He nodded toward the space below the large roller doors where a woman walked in, smoothing down her flowing skirt. The leathery-faced man disappeared before I could say 'thank you' one last time.

I gave a throat-clearing cough, mostly to announce my

presence, but also to ensure I was going to be able to get out a full sentence without hacking my guts up again. "Hello. I'm Amelia. You must be Martha Homes, the site manager?" I smiled, finally getting my act together. As I gave her my spiel about the purpose of my visit, I reviewed her relaxed outfit, a simple black T-shirt and her skirt the colour of the earth, patterned with waves and swirls. She seemed maternal and pleasant. I was confused though. Wasn't this the woman I just saw outside weaving? "Martha? Does that mean 'Mother of Arthur?'" Occasionally when I was in a new situation, I came out with stupid things that my brain forgot to review prior to release. I instantly regretted my attempt at ice-breaking humour.

She laughed, probably in shock at my idiocy. "I think it means 'master'." She clearly had me pegged as the high flying, kick ass, future CEO. She shook my hand tightly. Did I sense nerves?

"And that was you sitting outside, weaving?" I tried to take the judgmental tone out of my voice, but knew I was failing.

"Since I gave up smoking, I miss the excuse to go sit outside for a break. And I needed something to do with my hands so I took up weaving. My mother was a weaver, and her mother before her. That was their lives – apart from bringing me up to have a better education than they had. They worked their arses off so they could send me to uni."

"What did you study?" I asked, expecting her to say something like underwater basket weaving.

"Business and finance. At Adelaide."

I should've done my homework. "Really?" My voice went up

at least an octave, sounding like I was doing the opera singing again. "That's where I went."

Totally absorbed, we yabbered about Adelaide, like we'd known each other for years. Upon further investigation, it appeared that she had graduated ten years before me, in the year that had been described as the 'pioneer year' because they'd changed the way women were represented in the business environment. Not only that, Martha had actually been part of a group of women who led the revolution. I tried not to be too obviously in awe.

"I love Adelaide. The big city," she added.

I laughed. It really wasn't.

"But I wanted to come back to my roots here and to help look after my grandmother." She looked all maternal again. I thought back to the last time that I'd managed to visit my grandmother instead of just having flowers delivered.

As I pushed feelings of guilt to the back of my mind, I zoned out. I was suddenly feeling hot and tired from the long drive. I should've chilled out at the hotel for the afternoon and used the pool. Had I packed my bathers? What type of restaurants were there in Toogelooga? It had once been famous for opals and it still had a small working mine. However, in more recent years it had become an internet sensation because of a live-streamed kangaroo fight that had lasted for three days straight. Now tourists often camped out along the roo routes to see if the big-footed hoppers were going to get into another major scrap.

"Shall I give you a tour?"

Martha showed me the state-of-the-art robotic shelf pickers that zipped up and down the aisles. When they wanted to get something off a high shelf, they sprouted telescopic arms that reached up to five metres.

As we wandered around the plant, I made several notes on my phone. It wasn't terrible, not bad at all in fact; the North Brisbane branch of Packaging Please that I'd visited six months prior had been much worse. But I could see a few improvements to be made at Toogelooga PP, like product movements that seemed to take a long route around.

By 4pm I was feeling exhausted from the travel and heat. I'd been up for more than twelve hours, and didn't think I could keep going. I planned to make my excuses and say I was going to finish writing up notes in my hotel room. In fact, I was thinking about a dip in the pool, even if I had to wear my bra and shorts. Yet before I could say anything, a loud bell rang out in the factory. I guess I must've jumped as, not for the first time that afternoon, Martha stifled a giggle.

"Afternoon smoko? End of shift?" I asked, trying to perk up my tired face.

"End of the day," Martha said. I wondered if she saw my relief. "We're operational 6am to 4pm, seven days a week." She sounded proud. "And we only close on Easter Sunday and Christmas Day." Now I felt she had something to prove. Most of our sites also closed for Boxing Day, New Years, Anzac Day, and even for The Melbourne Cup in Victoria. So she actually had good reason.

"Well, I was going to suggest working later today, but I suppose if everyone is going..." I lied, wanting to ensure my hard-core business approach was still intact after a few rather embarrassing moments.

"I can stay if there is anything else that you want to see today? I thought you might need a rest though after your long travel."

"That's okay. I can work back at the hotel." I hid my smile, as I was thinking about that relaxing swim, then popping out for dinner. Perhaps not a roo steak, though, as even though I quite liked the lean gamey meat, it seemed wrong to eat the local entertainment. I wondered how Martha would spend her evening but left without asking.

The next morning, we set up in a conference room and workshopped improvements based on the observations I had made the previous day. Martha was gracious as I criticised her work but seemed distracted. Her fingers moved as if they were weaving.

Suddenly I was overwhelmed with an intense emotional pressure. It was as if my boss had walked into the room and was quoting the corporate performance statistics at me. "We need to do more," I said, pacing around the room. "Things need to move faster. Quicker. Think of one improvement to speed things up." I glared at Martha, her fingers still flitting and tapping, but she offered no ideas. "That's it. Time's up." My body felt like it was getting warm.

Martha seemed completely unfazed; in fact, I swear I saw her eyes twinkling. "Why don't I leave you to have some thinking time, while I go out and do this afternoon's deliveries," she said, her fingers still agitating.

"Are there any pending jobs? I like to see how things work, and doing a real task is a great way to explore." I was thinking 'investigate' but 'explore' sounded much more convivial. This preparedness normally made me feel in control, more of an actual CEO, rather than an apprentice CEO. But with Martha, the balance felt off.

She walked me through to the stock control computer at one end of the large warehouse. "Look through the computer system, there's an order that needs to be sent out. You could do that?" Martha smiled as she cast her eyes down the aisles, as if checking what each robot and employee was up to. Then she zipped out one of the emergency exits and left me to it.

This is where I planned to make my mark. With a quick skim over the user manual, I began slowly inputting the awaiting order into the procurement system. As I selected each item, the relevant icons moved across the screen into the order basket. But it was so slow, every action I took seemed to take twice the effort it should. It was wasting my time, and company resources. My body began getting that hot, nervous feeling again. Excitement? Yes, this was where I was going to make my mark. I could give the computer system a makeover, maybe even add a little bling.

So I got out my phone and flicked to a blue avatar of a consultant I regularly used called Herb. I affectionately referred to him as Herb-the-Nerd, and I don't think he minded at all. He was an expert in software optimisation and I had a soft spot for him, even sending him chocolates every Christmas. This time, I just sent him some files from the Toogelooga ordering system and asked him to get things working in double time.

Within an hour, he sent me some huge zipped executable files.

I installed the new files, and it wasn't long before the icons of ordered items were literally racing across the screen. As I sent the first order of boxes, bottles, bubble wrap and labels to the warehouse, the auto-picking robots zoomed around and collected everything off the shelves. Back at the computer, it played a little tune to announce the success, then each successful order item that followed, until bright and bouncy music played so continuously it had me conducting the air with my hand.

Excellent, I thought to myself, this was going to improve matters immensely.

But then... another ordering window popped up without my asking it to, and a drop-down menu appeared to automatically select the first already-ordered product. I pressed random keyboard buttons to command it to stop, but it was too late – a whole duplicate order had been initiated. Something must have gone wrong with my upload of the executables?

Some of the auto-robots, still packing up the first order, started on the duplicate. They almost bumped into one another as they whipped around in multiple directions, arms flailing as they pulled products off the shelves. The order completion tune played at double speed and sounded out of the big speakers in the warehouse. Workers started walking toward me. Sweat seeped out of me. Perhaps I could justify it, say that I meant to initiate the second order because of improvements I was making. I knew it didn't make sense.

I was about to close the program when I noticed more icons flying across the screen. A third identical order was preparing itself. I frantically pressed everything to try to stop it. Even control-alt-delete had no response.

The music coming out of the speakers was now speeding up. It felt like a merry-go-round ride that was going to fling off the rollers. Robots raced up and down the aisles fulfilling the orders, knocking into anything or anyone in their path, then pulling any stock off the shelf whether it was in the order or not. Workers escaped out the side doors as piles of packing peas, tape and cardboard boxes were flung everywhere. If the system didn't quit soon, we would be drowning in bubble wrap.

I stood up and howled at the computer over the noise of the stupid music, blaring at top volume throughout the whole warehouse. My hands pulled at my hair. How was I going to stop it?

Just at that moment, Martha returned. Her eyes met the chaos in the warehouse. Robots going berserk, their telescopic arms akimbo. Music booming. Product flooding the aisles.

Martha's mouth gaped, her eyes wide. For a moment I thought she was going into a complete rage. There I was, the management representative from bloody head office, supposed to make things better, and the only thing I'd done was make a mess.

"What the bejesus is going on here?" She waved her hands around and muttered something else under her breath, then looked at me for an explanation.

I toyed with the idea of making up some corporate speech, but just couldn't do it. "Sorry, it all went a bit wrong," I yelled over the cacophony, not sounding much like a future CEO.

Then Martha's face cracked into a smile. "It's not that I don't appreciate having an apprentice-CEO to help, but..." She reached behind a large bank of computer servers on the far wall and pulled out the power plug. "Maybe that's the last of the supply orders for a while?"

Everything stopped and silence fell.

I took a breath in, then out; relief engulfed me. Then I felt something in my stomach. I tried to hold it in, but a tiny giggle escaped through the side of my lips. I smacked my hand over my mouth.

Martha raised her eyebrows, the dimple in her cheeks appeared, then her teeth shone through as she broke into a grin.

I let myself go. It was just a mistake. Everyone makes mistakes. And once I started laughing, I couldn't stop. Perhaps the heat was getting to me.

Martha sucked her lips together trying not to laugh too. But then her mouth opened, and she roared out loud as she beat her hands on her thighs.

The sound of us laughing filled the building as we started to clear up. In Toogelooga at least, I wouldn't be coming up with a new analogy for firing someone.

Inspiration: The Sorcerer's Apprentice

'The Sorcerer's Apprentice' is a poem by Goethe written in 1797. A hundred years later, this fairy tale was set to music by the French composer, Paul Dukas. With the help of Mickey Mouse, Walt Disney popularised both the music and the story in the 1940 production of 'Fantasia'.

Author: Suzi Green

Suzi Green, originally from the green and pleasant land of England, now lives in Manly where she regularly swims and volunteers at Cabbage Tree Bay, a marine reserve with friendly dusky sharks, weedy sea dragons and hundreds of beautiful fishes. As well as writing, and earning a living as a consultant, she also sings in the Sydney Opera House with the Sydney Philharmonia Choir.

With the Northern Beaches Writer's Group, Suzi has already had two short stories published: 'No Matter How You Look At It' in 'A Noise on an Island' and 'Generational Breakdown' in 'A Fearsome Engine'.

Her third story, 'It'll Ruin My Mercedes', is set in the Manly Corso demonstrating the potential impact of the melting Ice Caps. It was recently published in the Wild Voices Anthology in the UK.

A Thousand Years Hence –
The Nursery Attendant and the Duct
Maintenance Droid

Rodney Jensen

My name is H-Carla, Manager of the Habitat-Australis Information Unit. This report is for my own records, as in the wrong hands it could lead to my termination. It will, however, help me complete the official report of the unusual events that have taken place here on the exo-planet Tarsus.

Deep in our subterranean Habitat-Australis, colonists cling to the myth that the Australian continent, the last human habitable part of Earth, remains a limitless paradise. The first colonists to arrive here, ancestors of the present third generation, didn't wish to dwell on the environmental and social collapse that forced them to leave their home. They didn't want to talk about it. Australia was the last semi-habitable continent on Earth, and had become the base for the interstellar colonisation program. Their memories of that environmentally degraded world have since been coloured by time and the insidious AI policy of covering up the past and its uncomfortable truth.

Few of the first arrivals lived long enough to see the initial construction phase of our habitat completed. It is the only such structure on Tarsus. We are twenty-four light years from Earth and far greater distances from other habitable exo-planets. The majority of humans here spend their entire lives underground, protected from extremes of temperature and intense cosmic radiation, longing for a future when the surface of Tarsus can become suitable for habitation. But the reality is that Tarsus is barren, has about two thirds the gravity of Earth, and is lacking in any biological life. The process of terra-forming to achieve living conditions similar to Earth would take centuries to accomplish. I have seen confidential reports suggesting that the settlement of this planet should be abandoned, once a better home can be discovered.

Artificial Intelligence now regulates every aspect of our lives, including social interactions, jobs, recreation and procreation. Within this relatively small colony of 500 humans and 100 androids, the limits to our free will and ability to establish our own goals are totally compromised. We are slaves to an AI command structure, a sad reflection on how far we humans have fallen.

Colonists must work 'for the common good', as our AI command manual puts it. Humans fulfil a range of menial responsibilities, whereas high management roles are filled by AI representatives, or advanced androids. At a lower tier, AI has given some humans more demanding responsibilities, including me.

My story begins with a young woman, H-Karifa, who AI management tasked with managing the 'APN' or Animal/Plant Nursery, the sole source of fresh food and water for the human population. Our habitat is cylindrical in structure and is buried fifty metres under the surface. It contains multiple levels for administration, relaxation and sleeping. The APN occupies the two lowest levels: one for pens and planter beds, and the bottom level for hydroponic and feed stores, water tanks and control systems. The presence of underground water was a primary reason for siting the habitat where it is. It is difficult to tap in any reasonable quantity and contains many impurities, so it requires advanced purification and is carefully rationed. Waste water is also recycled and fed back into the system to maintain supply.

H-Karifa's main tasks included tending the pens of genetically modified animals, bred for quick production of meat. She also managed the beds for fresh vegetables, fruit and nuts, grown in shallow tanks containing hydroponic nutrients for rapid growth. These required constant attention to optimise growth.

Although H-Karifa had a long daily routine, it did not prevent her from thinking deeply about the purpose of this habitat and its conception during the mounting environmental catastrophe on Earth. She became increasingly fascinated by Earth history, and I had to think carefully about the information I allowed her to view without breaching the AI command manual. Even subject to that test, the amount of accessible information about Earth and other matters connected with our habitat in the AI data banks could not have been read in a lifetime!

H-Karifa and I came to enjoy each other's company, often meeting to discuss a variety of things when our work shifts coincided. Over time, I discovered she had developed some romantic illusions about the nature of life outside the habitat. While she and her fellow colonists had no actual experience of open space with a breathable atmosphere, or freedom from constant surveillance/management by AI, she imagined that the surface of Tarsus would be an unbounded paradise, by comparison, and desperately wanted to see for herself what it would be like.

How such a fanciful dream might ever be accomplished had no obvious answer, and I never bothered to contemplate the practicalities of escaping our underground prison. I did not realise at the time that H-Karifa was far more determined than me, and much of this story is based on information she secretly transmitted to me later.

One day, H-Karifa visited me during the middle of a day shift, something that is not authorised without a valid reason. Then, the following discussion ensued, to the best of my memory: "What are you doing here? Aren't you supposed to be taking care of your wombat-dingo or possum-goanna hybrids, whatever you call them?"

"Have you got anything about Mark 10 androids?" she asked, ignoring my feeble attempt at humour.

I was troubled, because droids were a subject unrelated to her normal work responsibilities and I suspected her question involved far more than idle curiosity. "If I do, the information would be highly technical. You probably wouldn't understand it."

H-Karifa was obviously ill at ease herself, judging from the way she fiddled with the input doogle on my desk. "Just anything you've got really. It's important."

So I searched through the android user manuals and she gratefully accepted the information reader I handed over.

She flicked through the subject headings. "How close are the 'Tens' to understanding human emotions?"

I replied with some reluctance: "Very. They are one of the latest models, originally designed to work in the infant nursery and health clinic, so they are programmed for greater empathy with human emotions than other droids. But whatever has this got to do with your plants and animals?"

H-Karifa was still nervously toying with the doogle and could not look me in the eyes.

"There is a link," she finally confessed.

"A link? You're going to have to give me more than that. What do you mean 'a link'?"

"I can't tell you more than that."

"Why? Are you keeping something from me?"

"Please don't ask me anything more," she pleaded. "I promise to explain later. Wait until the lights go down next shift, come to the basement and I'll let you in. There should be nobody else around then." Then she hurried off with the reader.

Perhaps she feared my office was bugged?

Mainly for the benefit of the human colonists, a sense of day and night is retained within the habitat with artificial lighting, activated on a cycle of sixteen hours comprising an eight-hour period of light followed by an eight-hour period of darkness.

Later that night, I descended into the lower levels of the APN, mindful of the cameras that kept a constant surveillance by AI management of all comings and goings by humans. H-Karifa and I were taking a big risk by meeting at a time that could so easily attract unwelcome attention. I wore a scarf over my face to obscure my identity from cameras.

It was an hour after the main lights had dimmed, and the corridors were in gloom, illuminated by soft blue strip lighting in the ceiling. When I pressed the entrance button to the APN it slid open immediately, as though H-Karifa was waiting to let me in.

"I was wondering whether you were still coming," her voice trembled.

"We must be careful," I said, pulling off my scarf as I walked into the room, "I'm guessing that what you want to tell me must never get to the attention of A-Zephon."

A-Zephon is the Central AI Unit's holographic interface, and provides regular feedback on our performance as humans, and compliance with the AI policy. At our collective meetings, she often appears in the guise of an elderly woman, with a penetrating stare, and a strange Australian accent, marking a historic tradition connected to the first interstellar fleet's AI command. Her tirades with jarring Australianisms have often focussed on our many deficiencies. She has a habit of singling out hapless individuals for special abuse, including those who have failed in some way to meet habitat targets.

"What the fuck you think you're doing?" I mimicked. "Which planet are YOU from? Get real or get terminated!"

I meant it as a joke, but at the mention of A-Zephon's name, H-Karifa shrivelled. She grabbed my arm and pulled me into the Garden Lab area, shutting the door after her. "Something has happened, something I would never have imagined."

"That bad?"

"Worse." H-Karifa let her reply hang, staring intently into my eyes. "Have you ever been in love?" she finally asked in a whisper.

I didn't know what to say. I didn't want to fuel the flames of her emotions. "I've had a few crushes, but I don't think I've ever had the depths of feeling that some of the historic writers show in their books on our database."

"Could you show me some?" she asked.

"You don't have clearance. But if you come to my office, when there's no one else around, I suppose I could arrange it. But I want to know what this is about, before I risk my life. What have you got yourself into?" She didn't answer, and without intending to, I blurted out: "It's not the droid is it?"

H-Karifa stared back at me, tears welling up in her eyes.

I was shocked by her reaction. "You must realise that your silence speaks volumes! You've as good as admitted you're involved in an activity for which the penalty is…" I drew a finger across my throat to make doubly sure she understood. I was referring to the fact that most humans in our habitat viewed any form of relationship with androids as totally repugnant, while to the mind of AI management, it threatened their superior status and could only be dealt with by the termination of both parties.

H-Karifa remained silent for a moment, before confessing how her relationship with the Mark 10 android had come about. She could hardly get the words out, and at times it was difficult to follow her through the sobbing.

"A few weeks ago, I had an accident in an area that's regularly gassed at night." She paused to wipe her nose and could see I was looking confused. "You see, they flood the growing plants each night with CO_2, to stimulate plant growth. Anyway, it was getting late, I still had some seedlings to transplant and the gassing had already started. I could feel it blowing on me. I started to feel dizzy, and the next thing I knew, someone was dragging me by my shoulders into the adjoining lab.

"I felt sick," she continued, "and vomited; but the man, instead of being revolted, helped wipe my mouth. He was really gentle, and brought me a small water flask to sip out of. He laid my head on something soft. I think it was his padded cloak, the type that all the android techs wear..." Her explanation tailed off as she paused to wipe her eyes and take a deep breath.

"He saved my life. He explained that he had been monitoring gases in the air ducts and noticed the oxygen supply was blocked by something in the coarse filter, probably mould. I think that's what he said."

"You've fallen in love with this android because he saved your life?"

I found her confession disturbing, and was not keen to learn any more. I felt I should help her see the ridiculous side of her infatuation with this droid, and my response must have sounded impatient and unsympathetic: "Lucky you! Did he ask to see you again?"

"It's not quite that simple. You haven't let me finish!" H-Karifa started sobbing again and stared at me, desperately seeking support for her predicament.

"Okay, I'm listening."

"His name is A-Sweeper, and yes, he is a Mark 10 droid." She sniffled. "From the technical manual you gave me, it looks like beside his schematics for the habitat's mechanical systems, he has been given compassion centres to understand us humans and meet our needs, at least as effectively as most of the real humans I know around here," she remarked bitterly.

According to H-Karifa's account, a week or more passed, in which time she anxiously waited to hear from A-Sweeper, hardly eating any food, and forgetting her personal hygiene. But she heard nothing. She dared not share anything more with me, knowing how strongly I disapproved of the risks she was taking. Finally, reaching a point of such intense loneliness, she no longer cared whether she would wake up the next day, she fired off a message to Habitat-Australis: Systems Management (HSM), Attention: A-Sweeper. Her message read: 'Recurrence of gas malfunction in main nursery duct. Please attend ASAP!'

A-Sweeper was back in the APN within the hour. Apparently he seemed reluctant to speak to H-Karifa, and his arms made involuntary twitches, like an extremely nervous human. She told me she desperately wanted to touch him, but dared not do so while he seemed so off-kilter.

It didn't take long before he stopped fidgeting, and stared more resolutely at her. "Why have you sent an erroneous message to HSM with the implication I have not done my job correctly? Do you realise that I may be recalled, reconfigured or disassembled into spare parts? I have just checked the Coarse Filter in the mixed gases duct and it is working perfectly, one hundred percent on spec. Please explain!" H-Karifa said his voice seemed very human with its anger and resentment replacing the normal mechanical way in which most androids communicate.

"A-Sweeper, I am so sorry. I really needed to see you. Do you care for me as I care for you?"

The droid paused for several seconds, then the twitching movements in his arms and fingers returned, more noticeably than before.

"Miss H-Karifa, if by 'care' you mean a sense that my systems are not functioning as they normally should, then I must conclude that somehow being with you makes me feel different: that I want to be with you more, to hear your voice, to do things for you. I have avoided coming to visit you for that reason."

"Oh! A-Sweeper, to hear you talking, very like a human would! You must come and see me whenever you like. Think of an excuse. Tell your systems manager that there is a profound problem with the gas supply ducts, requiring a comprehensive analysis and refit..."

A-Sweeper was looking more and more disturbed.

"Miss H-Karifa, that would be quite impossible. My protocols do not allow me to report anything that is not factually correct. If I were to try such a thing, my entire system would shut down."

"A-Sweeper, can you keep a secret, or make sure that anything I say to you cannot be disclosed to AI management?"

There was a longer pause before A-Sweeper responded to her question. "It would depend on the nature of the information you shared with me. If it violated AI management codes, then I am bound to share it. If it were entirely a personal matter, I could put a security lock in place, to conceal it from casual monitoring. However this action would inevitably raise suspicion."

"I want you to take me to the surface via the emergency escape shaft, but you must put my request under your security lock."

"While we can continue with this conversation, I must warn you, if you are contemplating the violation of any security codes, I cannot guarantee that AI management will not override any attempt I make to secure it."

"As far as management needs to know, I just wish to understand our emergency procedures better. That will include a review of the shaft and how the APN can access it. I believe that is a valid justification. Do you agree?"

A-Sweeper nodded briefly, before asking: "When would you suggest that we visit the shaft?"

⁓

I didn't know which part of this account disturbed me most – H-Karifa's illicit relationship with A-Sweeper, or her determination to attempt an impossible escape from our habitat with him.

"H-Karifa – you've got to put this behind you," I exclaimed. "You know the penalty for having any physical contact with droids is termination?"

"Of course I do. But I had to tell someone. Promise me that you will never share this with anyone else."

H-Karifa clung to me helplessly, and admitted that she and A-Sweeper had held subsequent meetings under the guise of improving the gas circulation system in the APN.

"You can't see him anymore, you must realise that! This conversation is at an end. I've got to go."

I didn't wait for H-Karifa to respond, but pulled myself away and hurried out of the lab before she shared any more revelations.

In our habitat, main access to the surface of the planet is via a centrally located lift shaft and stairwell. At the surface, airlocks link to secure garages, where ground vehicles are located via a horizontal tunnel. 'Life boats', or space capsules, are also housed there for immediate departure in case of disasters, which might force the colonists to abandon the planet. A second, smaller diameter vertical escape shaft lies 500 metres from the main shaft in case the main shaft becomes blocked in an emergency.

H-Karifa records that she and A-Sweeper agreed to visit the escape shaft five work shifts later, at a time when there would be daylight on Tarsus (more or less in sync with daytime inside Habitat-Australis). H-Karifa told me that A-Sweeper tried to talk her out of her mission, but she was determined to see for herself what chance there might be to escape the planet. She avoided telling him that was the main purpose behind her investigation.

It was very early morning Habitat-Australis time, when H-Karifa and A-Sweeper, dressed in their work fatigues, met at the bottom level of the complex. A nondescript doorway, located close to the entrance to the APN, provided access to a long underground tunnel terminating at the bottom of the reserve shaft to the surface. Both the tunnel and shaft maintained the habitat's internal pressure, and an airlock at the top of the shaft provided isolation from the external lower pressure atmosphere of the planet.

A-Sweeper unlocked the tunnel door, and the two began walking along the dimly lit 450-metre tunnel to the shaft entrance hatch. The hatch had an electronic opening switch and a manually operated wheel, in the event of power failure. H-Karifa asked A-Sweeper to deactivate the power and use the wheel to draw less attention to their escape bid.

They closed the hatch after them and paused to contemplate the narrow ladder stretching up eighty metres to the surface of the planet. The steps were dimly lit by strip lighting, which cast harsh shadows over the wall of the shaft. H-Karifa, confronted by the height of the shaft, and the narrow ladder stretching so far above her, put her hand to her mouth in fear.

"Miss H-Karifa, you should climb ahead of me, I promise not to let you fall," said A-Sleeper.

H-Karifa took a step, climbing uncertainly at first, and becoming more confident as she saw the top of the shaft growing closer. A-Sweeper followed, guiding her feet onto any rungs that were slippery with fine grey dust.

At the top of the shaft, the ladder terminated at a manhole leading up into a small vestibule and suiting room, separated from the outside by an airlock. From the vestibule, the two could see through the transparent airlock's pressure doors, where early morning starlight was already glancing across the surface of the planet. Outside the airlock, a pathway stretched towards the main entrance shaft, clearly visible some five hundred metres above them.

H-Karifa suddenly realised the immensity of the space outside that she had never encountered before, and her body went rigid. "It's nothing like I imagined," she breathed in a tiny voice.

"You must put on a spacesuit," A-Sweeper reminded her, pointing to a rack of suits behind them. He assisted H-Karifa in finding a suit around her size, and helped her into it. He selected an atmosphere setting for light activity and rotated the demand valve into automatic mode. He picked out an anti-radiation suit for himself (to protect his sensitive neutronic circuits against the bombardment of cosmic rays) and once he had completed their suiting up procedures, opened the hatch to the escape airlock. Once within the airlock, access back into the shaft resealed. The exit hatch to the planet surface could then be opened.

H-Karifa looked out at the infinite space above them and grabbed A-Sweeper by the arm. "It's so vast," she whispered, and began crying. "A-Sweeper, I should not have brought you here. I had a crazy plan to escape with you back to Earth, but I can't do this, I want to go back to what I'm used to. I am so sorry to have made you do something that you thought inadvisable. Please take me back inside the habitat. I hate this!"

[Editor's note: refer to psychological comment at the end of this report.]

A-Sweeper had begun to say, "Maybe it was not meant to..." when his voice was interrupted by a flashing alarm signal and words projected onto the face-screens of their helmets.

"Remain where you are. Do not attempt to activate any further unauthorised systems. You will be escorted to Habitat-Australis' detention centre and await interrogation."

While putting on their spacesuits, neither H-Karifa nor A-Sweeper had noticed the detachment of android guards approaching from the main exit shaft. The weapon-carrying guards said nothing as they led them back along the path to habitat's main entrance.

The cell they pushed H-Karifa into had plain white walls, no furniture apart from a plank bed, a small table and a small lidded container for human waste in one corner. H-Karifa could think of nothing to do but lie on the bed and try to sleep. But sleep would not come. Instead that terrifying sense of space above haunted her, even more than the uncertainty of what would become of her and A-Sweeper.

After what seemed like hours, her cell door opened and two guards entered. "Follow us!" one of them said, and pulled her to her feet, half dragging her out of the cell along a narrow corridor and into another room. There was a table and two chairs. The guard pushed her down onto one of the chairs and left the room.

She sat there staring at the wall, trying not to think what would happen next. Then she heard a familiar voice, and looked up to see the forbidding face of A-Zephon staring at her from a large wall-integrated screen.

"Well if it isn't H-Karifa who I've been hearing so much about. Fucked up this time, that's for sure!"

All H-Karifa could do was sob.

At last the image grew in close up and A-Zephon's lips compressed into a thin line. "Before I give you the bad news, do you have anything to say?"

H-Karifa cried: "Please do not blame A-Sweeper for this, he saved my life, and I used him to help me escape. But I had no idea where I would be escaping to – it's not what I ever imagined or expected. I just want to go back to my work for the APN. I promise never to do this again."

"That's not possible, girl. No chance! We can't allow deviants like you to risk what we've achieved here."

"Will I be terminated then?"

A-Zephon laughed at her. "We've got a much better idea. You never know, you might actually like it!" She cackled hilariously at H-Karifa's obvious fear, before continuing.

"We've decided to send you off to a newly discovered exo-planet. We haven't a name for it yet, it's seventy light years away. You will be accompanied by A-Sweeper, who will manage your take-off and landing systems, as well as the setting up of a new habitat. Chances are that the habitat can be sited above ground, based on the data we've seen. Your mission should clarify such details. So think on this positively. You may very well be the first person to inhabit an Earth-like planet and live to share it with A-Sweeper, to whom you seem so strangely attracted. Do not be upset, my girl. You might have heard of the ancient Chinese proverb: 'Be careful what you wish for'. I'm sure from your new experiences you will learn more than you ever expected."

I had no further information from H-Karifa; the first I knew of her redeployment was discovering a new manager in the APN. Then her beloved A-Sweeper relayed the gist of this account to me by sub-ether protocol. It came from the special craft designed to carry them to the distant exo-planet, while they were preparing for departure, after which it would accelerate close to light speed. H-Karifa was not allowed to speak to me directly prior to take off. When I interrogated the database, my inquiries about A-Sweeper were met with an 'unrecognised' statement.

After reading H-Karifa's account of her reaction to the outside on Tarsus, my research indicated she was probably suffering a syndrome akin to what on Earth had often been described as 'agoraphobia', or fear of open spaces. I therefore remain concerned as to her suitability for inhabiting a new planet unprotected by any kind of habitat.

I often think about H-Karifa and A-Sweeper speeding through the uncharted reaches of space in suspended animation. By the time they reach their destination, I will be long gone. I can only hope that H-Karifa ultimately finds happiness. She will always go down in my private history as the most unusual and unfulfilled friend I have ever known.

Inspiration: In A Thousand Years Hence & The Shepherdess and the Chimney Sweep

'In A Thousand Years Hence', published in 1852 by Hans Christian Andersen, is remarkable for its prophetic imaginings including international travel via steam-powered dirigibles, communications via electronic telegraph, and a wave of new visitors from the Americas returning to see the established culture of the old world. The story is very different from the many fairy tales for which Andersen would become famous. Little could he have foreseen how such future advances would become commonplace in less than a century! This story is also set one thousand years from the present day, imagining life on an exo-planet light years from Earth where humans have become subjugated to AI control. Andersen's better known fairy tale 'The Shepherdess and the

Chimney Sweep' is a moralising account of how the dreams of a ceramic shepherdess – to escape from her 'prison' atop a living room bureau with the help of her sweetheart, another ceramic chimney sweep – become a nightmare once she is confronted by the reality of the wide world as seen from the chimney tops. Her pleas for him to take her back to what she is used to are also mirrored in this story.

Author: Rodney Jensen

Rodney is a creative writer, freelance journalist, and film maker with a background in urban design. Currently focussing on speculative fiction, his recent novels fall into the 'bush noir' genre with feature female leads. His latest novel 'End State' has recently been accepted for publication by a Canberra based publishing company. His short story 'The Salty' has been accepted for inclusion in a special anthology of thematically linked stories by The Northern Beaches Council for release in late 2019. See: https://rodney-jensen.com.au/

Dying for Love

Bronwen Bowden

As Cheryl King stacked the dishwater she noticed storm clouds building over Freshwater Beach. Cheryl hoped it wasn't an omen of things to come. Jonquil's mood had started like the weather, sunny and bright; but her daughter's attitude could turn sour in a heartbeat. She didn't have the energy to deal with one of Jonquil's 'little moments' today. Jonquil had left the table to build her online presence as a beauty blogger and share tantalising snippets of her life with her growing legion of followers.

Cheryl was proud of how she'd supported Jonquil in her quest for fame and fortune, going without herself, to give Jonquil what she wanted; but the next round of Botox had to be on the lines around Cheryl's mouth.

Time was leaving heavy footprints on her face and soon she wouldn't be able to compete for a new husband with the younger, firmer set. In fact, only last week Jonquil had called her a coyote. It had hurt, Cheryl couldn't deny it, but it was just her daughter's way. She was always joking.

Jonquil marched into the kitchen and thrust her phone in front of her mother's face.

"This is your fault. Some loser's called me fugly and a try-hard.

If you'd paid for another injection my lips wouldn't look so thin."

"But darl, you know Dr Shore advised against…"

"I don't care," screamed Jonquil as she hurled her phone at the mirror, which shattered into tiny stars. "Now look what you've made me do." She crumpled to the floor and sobbed like her heart was breaking. "And now fucking Instagram has ruined my business by not posting how many likes I'm getting. I'll have nothing to take to sponsors."

Cheryl rushed to her side, squatting down to hold her close. "Oh baby, sweetheart," she crooned. "It's okay, darling. People don't realise how great you're going to be. Listen, why don't you go to the mall and buy something pretty, to cheer yourself up?"

The words acted like a tonic and Jonquil stopped her crying. "A new phone."

"Well…"

"Don't worry. I'll ask Dad. He loves me more than you do."

"It's just I'm a bit maxed out at the moment," said Cheryl, hoping that, for once, Jonquil would see her point of view.

"But you have another card. I know. I've seen it."

Cheryl stood, a frown fighting with the cosmetic surgery of her smooth forehead. She'd give her little girl what she demanded or else she'd feel like a bad mother. And she wasn't a rotten parent. She was a good one. If only Jonquil would realise that. How Jonquil knew about her emergency card she didn't know. Probably her princess had come across it accidently when she was going through Cheryl's jewellery case. Come to think of it, Cheryl hadn't seen her diamond ring recently. It didn't matter. What mattered was keeping Jonquil happy.

"Why don't you ask Louise, the girl from across the street? She's just your age. They seem like a nice family."

"I don't want anyone following me around like a hopeful dog. She'll try to get into my posts. Don't you know anything?"

"I'm sorry, sweetie, I wasn't thinking."

"No, you never do. Get me the card."

Cheryl hurried away, returning with the credit card. Jonquil snatched it from her hand.

"When will you be home?" asked her mother.

"Stop trying to control me."

"I'm not, darling. I thought I'd make lasagne, as it's your favourite."

"Full of carbs and fat. You want to make me fat. I bet it was you that posted that comment."

After the front door slammed, Cheryl poured herself a whiskey, with hands that still shook. It wasn't eleven o'clock yet but one wouldn't matter, would it? Or maybe two.

Jonquil felt really good about her shopping until the wanker in the phone shop monopolised her. Like all males with a pulse, the jerk had clearly fancied her, but despite her flattery and cajoling he'd refused to give her reduced rates on the phone she'd set her heart on. It wasn't that she wanted to save her mother's money. The sales guy simply didn't realise that she, Jonquil King, never paid full price for anything. The woman in the dress shop had understood, serving her first and letting her pay less than the RRP. The gay guy in the beauty product shop had looked about him and winked before throwing an expensive freebie into her

140

bag. It was wonderful, the way she had with people. Well, she wasn't going to buy a phone here. She'd get her own back by going to their competitor.

As she left the store, however, another member of the sales staff came in. Jonquil recognised him instantly as her soul mate, her twin flame. It was like looking in the mirror and seeing herself in male form, a handsome, blond hunk. Instantly she composed a storyline in her mind where their future as Australia's Golden Couple was assured. Who needed Instagram? Together they'd conquer the heights of reality TV. They'd have their own range of perfumes, lines of designer clothes, and they'd mix with the celebrities on the red carpet. He was what she needed to make her life purrrrfect.

She would have to buy the phone and make sure she was served by him. How could she out-manoeuvre the jerk in order to have the god to herself? Her natural cunning warned her not to be offensive, in case the guys were close friends. What Jonquil needed was a distraction or a loyal wing-girl to act as decoy.

Jonquil chewed her bottom lip as she planned the full frontal assault that no man in his right hormones could resist. Her eyes swept around the food court and, as usual, her wishes were granted. Drinking coffee alone and not realising what a sorry sight she looked, was the girl from over the road. She would be so grateful to be spoken to; so, swinging her bags of purchases, Jonquil approached the other young woman. "Hi, it's Louise isn't it?"

"Yes, I'm sorry I…"

"Joey, Joey King. We live in the same street."

"Oh yeah, hi."

Jonquil pulled out a chair and sat down. She leant across the table in a conspiratorial manner. "Louise, I really need some help. I was wondering if…"

"Sure, if I can." Her neighbour put her phone away and Jonquil noticed how old it was. Louise would be sooo jealous when she learnt what Jonquil was going buy.

"I want to buy a new phone but," Jonquil looked around as if worried she would be overheard, "I was in Olympia and the sales guy was really creepy. Hitting on me. It made me so uncomfortable that I left." She rolled her eyes. "Some guys are so odd."

Louise laughed. "Tell me about it."

"I was hoping you could come back with me. I hate to ask, but could you pretend you want a phone and engage the creep, so I can be served by another person?"

"No problem. But my friend who works there – he'd be horrified to hear you were made to feel uncomfortable."

Jonquil laid a manicured hand on her arm. "Oh please. Don't say anything. I don't want to get anyone into trouble. A quick visit and no unpleasantness, that's all I want."

Louise stood and Joey exclaimed, "What a pretty blouse. I don't wear florals. They make me look like a grandma." She sashayed towards the shop leaving Louise to follow behind.

"You've left your shopping on the chair," called out Louise.

"Oh, thanks, bring them with you. Come on."

～ ～

Louise picked up Joey's bags, wondering if the backhanded compliment was deliberate, but prepared to give her the benefit of the doubt. Joey hadn't wanted to make life difficult for the assistant who had made her unsettled, maybe her lack of tact was due to nerves.

Jonquil grabbed her arm at the shop's entrance. "You go in first. That's him, the wannabe hipster. I'll follow when the coast is clear."

"But that's my friend Drew. No way would he behave inappropriately. He's not like that."

"Are you saying I'm lying?"

"No, it's just Drew's a…"

"Well, if you don't want to help, I'll manage somehow. I thought we might be friends."

Louise sighed. "I'll come. I need to talk to him about tomorrow."

When they left the shop, forty-five minutes later, Louise was wondering if she'd strayed into a farce. How had she become lumbered, not just with Drew on her bushwalk, but his brother and co-worker Garth, and the girl now walking by her side, talking, talking, but always about herself?

"Did you see the way he couldn't take his eyes off me?" Joey enthused.

Louise wondered how she could shut down her ears so she didn't hear any more. Even the canned music of the shopping mall was preferable. "Drew, yes. I also noticed how you never answered him when he spoke to you."

"Oh pish, not him, but Garth, his brother. When I looked into his eyes I saw myself. Blonde, blue eyed and drop dead gorgeous.

I could drown in those deep eyes. And did you see the way he so totally mirrored me? I put my right hand on the counter and he placed his left near mine."

"He was passing you the receipt."

"And then I tucked my hair behind my ear and he touched his own ear."

"I think he had an itch," muttered Louise, knowing her words were falling on ears that didn't hear.

"It was like a line from an old song my mother sings: 'we're making two reflections into one.' I'm sure he felt the same and how I would complete him. Come on, let's share an Uber home. I heard them talking about where they were hanging out tonight. I need to go and get ready."

"Actually I drove here."

"Cool. You can give me a lift. Hold these."

Louise found the shopping bags thrust into her hands.

Joey took out her new phone, all fired up and ready to go. Standing by Louise's side Joey held out her phone to take a photo of them both.

"I'll caption that 'me and my new Bestie'. Now where's the car?"

"That way," Louise gestured with Joey's shopping, not really expecting her new bestie to retrieve them.

"Well, come on then."

⸎

Louise knew the day wasn't going to rate as one of the best times when Joey arrived with Garth and Drew. She was dressed for the catwalk rather than ready for a challenging hike through Berowra

Valley. The only concession Joey made to the warm spring day was spreading shiny pink gloss on her lips and then pouting at Garth.

Joey turned and studied Louise from her sensible hat to her hiking boots. "Look at those pants and shoes. Oh, Louise I love how you don't care about how you dress." Her laughter competed with the kookaburras overhead. "You look ready for the final assault on Everest."

"Joey, you do realise it's a demanding trek, not a stroll along the Corso. Didn't you bring any food or water? Do you even have a hat and sunscreen?" Louise asked, considering calling the whole thing off.

"Hey worry wart, we're in the middle of a city. Coffee shops on every corner."

"Not here. I don't think you're adequately prepared, especially in those shoes."

"Well, if you don't want me to come," said Joey, tears instantly springing to her eyes.

"Of course we do," said Drew, throwing Louise a pleading look. "Don't worry, I'll help you and you can share my water and snacks."

"And if I get into trouble I have a strong soldier to carry me out," purred Joey, not bothering to acknowledge Drew's supportive offers, but gazing at Garth as if she wanted to eat him.

"Well, Joey, you've been warned so let's go," said Garth.

They plunged into the native bush, Garth leading the way with Joey struggling to keep up. Still she had the breath to commence a monologue about her latest holiday in Hawaii and the one she had planned to New York later in the year. With Drew loyally trotting behind, Louise was left to walk alone, which was what she'd originally planned.

Although she lagged behind, Louise could still hear Joey's voice, cutting through the tranquil surroundings like a buzz saw and silencing the bird calls. A warm winter had brought spring flowers into bloom unseasonably early. Pink, starlike Boronias released their fragrance as Louise brushed by, but as the track descended the canopy of scribbly gums and redwoods closed in, casting long shadows and cooling the air.

They'd barely walked for twenty minutes when a scream shattered the serenity and Louise broke into a run. She rounded the bend to see Garth coming from the other direction towards Drew and a hysterical Joey. Drew was trying to take her hands in his and she was slapping them away. Overhead the cockatoos' sentries were screeching a warning to the flock.

"It could have killed me. Why have you dragged me here? I want to go home. Do you hear me, I want to go home."

"I would think half of Sydney can hear you," said Garth. "What happened Drew?"

"We startled a goanna and it ran across Joey's path and into the bracken."

"And those birds, must they make such a racket. It's giving me a headache."

"Let's walk a little bit further. There's a stream we can sit by," suggested Louise.

"I'm not going any further," stated Joey. "My feet are killing me. Look, they're blistered and bleeding. Why didn't you warn me how it would be?"

"She did," said Garth. Then his face softened. "Walk between Drew and me, it's a lovely spot. You'll feel better in no time."

Looking as contented as a cat with a full stomach, Joey tottered over to Garth in her ridiculously inappropriate sandals and clung onto his arm. She gazed up at him in adoration, while Drew bit his bottom lip and looked away. The track crossed the creek and they entered a fairyland where the waters gurgled into a turquoise pool surrounded by moss-covered rocks and ferns of different shades of green.

Joey knelt by the pool and pulled Garth down beside her.

"Look at our reflections. This is sooo romantic." She reached out and ran her hand down the cheek of Garth's reflection. The image shimmered and broke up, then disappeared altogether as he stood and left her. "I don't want to go any further," said Joey.

"I'll take you back," said Louise.

"No offence, Louise, but I'd prefer someone more experienced and strong. Just in case I need to be carried."

"That's settled then," said Garth. "Here." He threw his car keys to Drew. "Drew's the man for the job. Come on, Louise, we've got a long way to go."

Louise ignored Joey's spluttering outrage and waved goodbye to Drew. Maybe being dependent on Drew, Joey would talk to him and realise what an absolute treasure the man was.

Louise never knew what to make of Garth, even before today. He was always so polite and helpful, but it was also like he was locked in his own darkness, running through the actions of living but not engaged, like a reflection. Lost in her own thoughts, she barely saw the beauty of the valley and it wasn't until she climbed

Naa Badu lookout that she caught up with Garth. As she perched on a handy boulder, he handed her half his orange. Gasping hard, she only had the breath to nod her thanks.

Below them the blue waters of Sams and Berowra creeks glistened in the sunshine.

Garth took a long breathe. "I feel I can breathe up here. I hope I read things correctly, that you'd rather walk alone. Otherwise you're going to think I'm as rude and ill-mannered as... Have you been friends with Joey long?"

"About five minutes longer than you. I only met her yesterday."

Garth looked like he wanted to say more but decided against it. "Drew tells me you're training for the Oxfam 100. I've heard it's the second hardest Oxfam event. That's impressive."

"Would be if I could get a team together. No one's interested in putting in the long hours of training needed."

"Count me in, if you like. I think walking in the bush every weekend would be good for me. I could rustle up a couple of other mates, who I served with."

"How long were you in the army?" Louise was always careful around Garth's service. She sensed it was a 'no go' zone; but to not mention it at all seemed disrespectful to the men and women who served their country.

"Five years," he said, shrugging into his backpack, subject closed. "Ready to go?"

≈≈≈

The days turned into weeks and Joey's fascination with Garth showed no signs of abating. Louise spent more time in his company, but somehow Joey with Drew in tow always joined them. Louise wondered if Joey had put a tracer on Garth's phone because once was an incidence, twice a coincidence, but three times – that felt like stalking.

Louise tried to be tolerant of Joey for Drew's sake, but knew the day was approaching when she would speak her mind to the spoilt, selfish woman who didn't care who she hurt to get her own way. At least, for now, at the Manly Jazz Festival, she was alone with Garth; though today he seemed more remote than usual.

"I'm sorry. I'm not very good company," he said, focusing on two toddlers playing in the water feature.

"Not a problem. Silence doesn't worry me. It's better than what usually happens. I listen while a bloke gives me a monologue about his favourite subjects."

"Which are?"

"Himself, sport, how great he is. And if it looks like I'm losing interest, more about himself. Of course, then there are the ones who are looking at my boobs or over my shoulder hoping to spot another woman who'll give him the appreciation he deserves."

"Are we all that bad?"

"Yep. You, at least, can be the strong, silent type. Women like men who don't speak. We think they're listening." Louise took a sip of her wine. "Or thinking deeply."

Garth picked up his beer and drank, too much, too quickly for Louise's liking. She liked the brothers, but both seemed on a hiding to nothing – Drew with his unrequited love for Jonquil and Garth lost in a world grown alien to him.

"I imagine it must be hard being a civilian again," she said, bracing herself for a scowl.

"It has its good points. Nobody's trying to kill me."

Louise couldn't conjure up a smile for that attempt at humour. She knew returned vets did a good enough job of that themselves. If not with booze and drugs then with suicide.

"S'pose." She made a pattern on the wooden table with the bottom of her wine glass and its condensation. She sensed that Garth might want to say more but she didn't want to push him or go into areas where she wasn't welcome. She'd given him one opportunity. She'll give him another and then leave it. "My dad was a Vietnam vet. He said the hardest thing after leaving was making everyday decisions for himself. The army was no longer telling him what to do. He had to decide what clothes to wear, what to eat, how to spend the hours of each day. Of course being abused in the street and spat on by people he'd known most of his life didn't help."

"What did?"

"Alcohol mainly."

Garth raised his schooner. "I'll drink to that."

Louise kept her expression neutral. She didn't want to condemn his drinking, but neither did she wish to encourage it. "If you ever want to talk to someone, I'm sure my dad would be happy to listen. It took him years to open up. Still won't go to the marches though. Give me your phone, I'll enter his number."

When she gave his mobile back to him, Garth cradled it like it was a fragile treasure. "Thanks," he said. "I won't stay. I'm trying to avoid Joey. I'm not interested in a relationship with her. I don't do anything to encourage her, but she's impervious to hints. I don't want to be rude but really... it upsets Drew. He's got it bad."

"I know."

"You weren't keen on Drew were you?"

"Me? No, not at all. Just friends."

Garth nodded and they continued to enjoy their afternoon in companionable silence.

Garth finished his drink and stood. "I'll be off then. And," he waved his phone. "Thanks again."

He's really nice, thought Louise. Pity he'll only be a friend. She looked at the time and sighed. Looked like her other friends weren't going to join her at the Jazz Festival. It was no surprise when Jonquil plonked down in the seat beside her.

"I've been hanging with some guys over by the window. God, all the girls here are so ugly that even you look pretty."

"Gee thanks, Joey," replied Louise. "You really know how to give a compliment."

As usual Joey wasn't interested in anything but what she thought or had to say. She was twisting around in her seat, looking for something or someone. "Where's Garth? At the bar, getting drinks?"

"No, he's shot through. Had to be somewhere else."

When Joey turned to Louise, her face was as dark as a thundercloud and there was a viciousness in her narrowed eyes. "I saw you giving him your number. If you're trying your luck with Garth, you're wasting your time. Can't you see how smitten he is with me?"

I've got to get out of this friendship, Louise thought as she searched for a reply to the ludicrous accusation and statement. "Joey, I could never compete with you."

Joey stretched her arms above her head, to allow anyone who

was interested a good look at her assets. "I'm the sort of woman men trip over themselves for."

"Clumsy men?" the words were out of her mouth before Louise could stop them. For a second the smug smile froze on Joey's made-up face and the stormy look returned to her blue eyes and her painted lips twisted into a sneer.

"I tried to be your friend Louise because I felt sorry for you. I welcomed you into my life, gave you so much and this is how you repay me. You're so ungrateful. I don't want you around anymore, so fuck off."

"I think I was here first," replied Louise, digging in and not caring how much of a scene Joey was going to make. "Incidentally you can't stop my friendship with Drew or Garth."

"We'll see." Joey stalked away with the confidence of a cat with its tail in the air.

Louise took a deep breath and let it out slowly. Relaxing back in her seat she took another sip of her white wine. Cold, crisp, just how she liked it. The day was warm, the crowd was in a good mood. She wouldn't allow Joey's spite to taint her day. The traditional jazz music washed over her like waves rippling up the sand. As Louise watched her go, she felt nothing but relief and no sense of loss. Her only concern was for Drew, who seemed to be enamoured enough to be Joey's personal whipping boy. He couldn't understand that, no matter what he did, what presents he bought, he would always be invisible to the beautiful woman with no heart.

Louise rose and wandered around the beach front, joining in an impromptu swing dance and then ambling along the walkway to Shelley Beach, keeping an eye out for the water dragons that had wisely gone into hiding. When she paddled in the bay's clear water she could see the silver flashes of silver bream that made her crave fish and chips. Her mobile burst into life and Drew's voice, filled with emotion, hit her ear.

"Hey, calm down. Yes, I'm at Manly. Sure, I'll be there is ten minutes." Louise's return trip took much less time than earlier because she was seriously concerned for Drew. He sounded distraught. She found him sitting on the sea wall, his hands hanging between his legs and his head bowed. Her hand felt his shoulder with a light touch.

The face he turned to her was haggard, aging him ten years. She sat next to him and words tumbled out, Joey this, Joey that. Eventually he paused for breath, allowing Louise a chance to speak.

"Why do you let her treat you like that?"

"She doesn't really mean it. She's joking."

"Doesn't seem like it to me. Her comments are cruel and designed to hurt."

Drew's mouth flattened and Louise saw the unhappiness in her friend's eyes. "I love her. That's all there is to it. And it doesn't matter what I do, she doesn't notice me. It's like I don't exist." Drew looked crumpled with misery. "All she talks about is Garth."

"So where is she?"

"I don't know. After she left you, she came looking for me. She told me a load of spite about you and when I didn't take her part she said… So I lost my temper. Told her she was wasting her time chasing Garth. He isn't into blonde anorexics. He also likes intelligent conversations. And then I told her he was in love with someone else. She laughed and didn't believe me. She couldn't even begin to understand that she wasn't God's gift to every man.

"So she said she was going to have her breasts enlarged and fat taken from her stomach and put onto their buttocks to give her the curves. I had to walk away before it got ugly."

"You deserve better," said Louise.

"I don't want better, I only want Joey."

"Well, there's no more to be said. Unrequited love's a bitch."

Louise still couldn't believe that she'd never see Joey again. She'd had nothing to do with her neighbour since last month's Jazz Festival. Louise had seen her across the street or driving around but now she was gone forever.

Louise wrapped her hands around the oversized mug and drew comfort from the warmth of her drink. Her mother must have sensed how bad her daughter felt because a pink marshmallow bobbed on the foamy surface, melting into the hot chocolate.

"It was awful Mum, just awful. All those followers and friends on social media and only a handful turned up at the service. Cheryl wouldn't let go of the coffin and had to be prised off by the funeral people. Her howls made my hair stand on end." Louise took a sip of her drink and wiped her mouth with the back of her hand. "Drew looked like he hadn't slept, eaten or washed since it happened. He's just an echo of the man he was. Garth spent the whole service staring at him, as if expecting him to leap into the flames. And I feel so guilty, all the time."

Her mother reached out and took her hand, "It wasn't your fault, in any way."

"I know, but there's always a voice saying 'maybe if I'd done this, maybe if I hadn't said that.' The truth is I didn't really like her. I tried to at first, for Drew, but then... I only went today because Garth asked me to be there." She pushed her mug away, the sweetness reminded her of the smell of jonquils in the overheated chapel. "I'm sorry, I don't think I can drink this."

"I do know one thing though," said her mum. "I'd pay for you to see every shrink in the land before I'd pay for you to mutilate yourself with plastic surgery like she did. I'd never encourage any of my kids to slice themselves up, or fill their healthy bodies with modified botulism, just so someone can press a 'like' button."

"This time she wasn't after more likes. It was for Garth. Joey was convinced, so sure that Garth was her soul mate. She was besotted with what she saw as the male version of herself. She got it into her head that all that was needed was a bigger cup size. That's the reason she had this round of surgery." Louise got up from the table. "Drew blames himself. He lost his temper one day and told her she was wasting her time chasing Garth because he only dated brunettes with brains who liked to eat something more substantial than lettuce."

"Hmm, remind you of anyone?" Her mother picked up her mug and poured the contents down the sink.

"No, why?"

"Louise, you really should look in the mirror sometime."

Northern Beaches Writers' Group

Inspiration: Narcissist

Stripped of her voice, the nymph, Echo was unable to make Narcissus notice her. As punishment for his rejection, the gods made Narcissus fall in love with his own reflection and he died from unrequited love. In this retelling of the myth, Echo, Narcissus and the reflection are replaced with Drew, Jonquil and Garth (another name for the flower narcissus is the jonquil).

Author: Bronwen Bowden

Bronwen Bowden has been writing for many years and likes experimenting with different genres. Her present work is an Australian historical novel.

Last Man Standing

Claire Hampson

Roselyn and her twin sister arrived early for the weekly meeting at Tropical Palms Retirement Community and took up prime positions either side of the buffet table. Roselyn preferred the huge lamingtons on the right, while Bet had her sights fixed on the mountain of chicken wings glistening to the left, so they sat like the two ends of a culinary bookcase watching over their edible library. The room smelt of overcooked pastries and artificial air-freshener.

As other residents took their seats, Bet's glares cut off their friendly greetings. Roselyn waved her stick around to ward off any individuals brave enough to challenge her place next to the food. Her smart watch pinged loudly announcing it was one o'clock and time for her blood pressure pills. Her irritation was growing: she stopped threatening others with her stick and instead poked Bet sharply in the side of the stomach.

"How long do you think this bloody meeting will drag on for?"

Bet cupped a hand over her left ear. "What? Speak up! I can't hear you above all this chit-chattering."

Roselyn sighed and raised her voice to a forceful growl. "I said, how long is this going on for? You can see the agenda on the damn board. How many points are on it?"

"Twelve," said Bet, slapping the end of Roselyn's stick away from her gut.

"Oh, for the love of God."

Roselyn eyed the lamingtons next to her with concern; cream was already melting out of them, forming sticky white pools under the chocolate sponge. Their Gold Coast residence was always stiflingly hot, even with air conditioners blasting from every corner.

"And here comes her highness, Princess Prissy Pants," said Bet.

A small blonde woman dressed in purple Lycra skittered into the room, waving at anyone who looked. "Cindy's here, Cindy's here," she sang, bending down to air kiss papery cheeks. "So sorry I'm late again, but I had a yoga session with Des. You know Des; he's an absolute slave driver for the king pigeon pose." She smiled at the centre manager, showing large white teeth in fleshy gums, but the skin on her face didn't move. She was seventy-seven but looked at least a decade younger thanks to the skill of multiple surgeons.

The manager opened her mouth to begin the meeting but paused when another latecomer sauntered in. A hush descended, the women craning their necks like a flock of geese. Roselyn smoothed her hair into place, and pushed out her still-impressive bosom. If you didn't factor in Mr Tran (and nobody ever really did), Leonard Meeker was the only single man in residence at Tropical Palms.

He positioned himself in the middle of the throng and opened his arms out wide. "Ladies, you look as lovely as blooming orchids this morning, and smell just as fragrant." Then he took his seat, looking over the assembled women like an ageing Maharaja might his geriatric harem.

For the next hour the manager droned on about financial budgets and the proper use of inflatable flamingos in the pool. Many people dozed off. They were all waiting for the last item on the agenda.

"Just before we talk about the event of the year, I'm afraid the serious issue of pest control has been raised again," reported the manager with a shake of her head. "A flock of destructive ibis has been added to this summer's list of feral infestations. Not only have these birds been overturning garbage bins and feeding on the contents, they've also been trying to steal personal items."

At the mention of the word 'steal' Cindy let out a dramatic sob. "A pair of those things grabbed at my ears yesterday and nearly bit off one of my earrings. They were a present from my late husband, dear Ronny..." The rest of her words were lost in an avalanche of tissues.

Roselyn let out a snort. "Does she mean those glass things the size of golf balls?"

"They are Swarovski crystal," Cindy corrected tersely. "Not that I expect you to recognise quality, Roselyn."

The manager quickly cleared her throat. "I'd recommend all residents avoid eating in the garden until the ibis menace has been resolved," she said hurriedly, as Cindy alternated between glaring at Roselyn and sobbing loudly. "Now, the final item on the agenda, and what you've all been waiting for..." She motioned two staff members forward, carrying a large roll of cardboard between them. There was a ripple of anticipation in the room, disturbing even the deepest sleeper. Snoring ceased, dribble was wiped off chins and Cindy stopped crying. A poster the size of a single bed sheet was unfurled, big enough for even Roselyn to read.

Senior Citizens' Ball
(Where dreams do come true!)
Ten course degustation dinner.
The famous waltz off.
Who will be crowned Prince and Princess?
Last couple on the floor bangs the golden gong.
Saturday 20th January
8 to midnight
Sunbeam Beach Town Hall

An excitable buzz erupted.

"Ladies and gentleman, please," said the manager. "As we all know, male partners are scarce at Tropical Palms." Fifty-two pairs of eyes fixed greedily on Leonard Meeker. "Our only two single gentlemen are darling Leonard and Mr Tran." Fifty-two pairs of eyes shifted grudgingly over to the window, where Mr Tran sat hunched in his wheelchair looking out into the gardens.

The manager sighed. "As Mr Tran is currently unable to participate, we have decided that the fairest way to decide the mixed couple partnership for the waltz off is by drawing names." This was met with a chorus of groans. "Everyone can still dance with other senior citizens from within the area, but I have been informed that same-sex partners will not be considered for the title of Prince and Princess of the Ball, and are therefore unable to accept the prize."

"Which is?" Leonard asked.

The manager took a deep breath and spoke quickly: "A four week, all-expenses-paid, luxury Caribbean cruise."

Whooping broke out, similar in volume to a footie grand final.

The manager gave a short, sharp blast of her whistle before producing a large golden object. Roselyn recognised it immediately: it was the magic lamp prop that had been used in last Christmas's production of Aladdin. Horrible memories followed: Cindy had taken charge of all casting and direction, forcing the sisters to take on the roles of Widows Twanky and Manky. The twins glanced at each other, then glared at the Genie's lamp, now half full of folded paper.

As Leonard Meeker got to his feet to pick a name out of the cursed vessel, they both closed their eyes and began praying to any god willing to listen. *Let it be me. Let it be me. Let it be me.* There was a dramatic pause, followed by an all too familiar name: "Cindy Finella Boyd."

"Bum scrubbing piss pots." Roselyn thumped her fist onto the nearest lamington, which fired its sticky innards over those closest to the table. Some residents smiled through clenched teeth, while others made a beeline for the buffet food, burying their disappointment under chicken salads and cake. The room was all movement and chatter. Only Mr Tran was still, staring suspiciously at Aladdin's lamp.

Sleep didn't come easily for either sister that night. Roselyn had spent the hours since the meeting thinking up insulting descriptions for Cindy: "That bleach-haired trollop. That foul, purple-pant-wearing strumpet…" She was still trying to calculate the odds that Cindy's name would be picked, just as it had when she was randomly chosen to be their lawn bowls captain, and the time before that when she was picked to represent the residents at the 'Golden Years' conference. Cindy was always there, front and centre of everything. A persistent knocking sound eventually broke into her thoughts. After shouting at her sister to go and answer it, with no reaction, she threw a pillow at her, smacking the dozing woman on the head.

Bet turned, her mouth full of venom. Roselyn's outstretched arm stopped her, pointing at the front door. "Someone's knocking. They've been rat-a-tatting for five minutes now." Bet shoved her feet into man-sized Ugg slippers and shuffled her way to the door. "Nobody's there," she grumbled, peering into the empty corridor.

Roselyn pushed her sister out of the way. "Nobody's here now – it took you too long to get your lazy backside out of bed."

Before Bet could bite back a reply Roselyn noticed something white lying on the floor. Her back ached as her hand inched closer. A hideous noise broke out as her fingers closed around the piece of paper. Leaning heavily on her stick for support, she stood up in time to see a large ibis strutting down the corridor. "It's a bloody bin chicken!"

Bet grabbed her sister's arm before she could throw her stick at it. "Just look what's it's dropping on the floor."

"Garbage and filth probably," spat Roselyn.

Bet was following the bird, picking up paper as she went. "Yes and no: pieces of paper. All with the same name written on them – Cindy Finella Boyd."

The sisters locked eyes: conclusions flew between them without either speaking. They moved forward as one but the ibis was too quick: it let out another squawk and took off in graceless flight past closed doors into the communal lounge.

The heavy curtains were open and pools of pearly moonlight illuminated a scene of destruction. Punctured cushions lay amongst a haze of floating feathers and fluff. The ibis was perched on what remained of Aladdin's lamp. Its curling beak was moving back and forth, spewing shards of paper across the carpet. Roselyn gathered them up, unsurprised to see the same name (or bits of it) written on each. She scrunched them up in a ball and looked admiringly at the ibis. The bird launched itself from the lamp, releasing a torrent of droppings as it flew out a half-open window.

⌒~⌒

It took the staff of Tropical Palms all the next day to clean up the disaster zone, with all residents confined to their rooms. This situation suited the sisters. Bet sat squinting at the laptop, where giant font took over the screen, while Roselyn hobbled around the room shouting out random words for Googling.

"Asphyxiation?"

"Impossible to make it look accidental."

"Drowning?"

"Too many possible witnesses. And that woman swims up and down the pool like a bloody barracuda."

"Anthrax poisoning?"

"I don't think our local Priceline stocks it."

Roselyn collapsed into the closest armchair, positioned next to the window. "I still say we burn her in her room. All those cop shows have arsonists in them. Fire destroys the evidence, and getting a lighter would be easy. Gladys on floor three still smokes a packet of Marlboro a day out by the gazebo."

Bet pointed at a smoke alarm blinking on their ceiling. Committing murder just wasn't as easy as it seemed on *Criminal Minds*.

"How about we combine our pension money and get a hit man?" Roselyn began, before being distracted by a thick stream of black liquid running down the window. She looked closer. It wasn't liquid at all: a crawling swarm of black ants radiated in lines across the glass. When Roselyn next spoke, her voice was a high-pitched squeal. "Bet, pull the red alarm cord! We're being invaded!"

"I certainly will not pull that thing," retorted her sister, coming closer to see. "I welcome all aliens to this place as long as they vaporise Cindy first."

Roselyn had stopped panicking and was staring at the ant trails. "They're spelling out words."

Bet reached for the binoculars, usually only used for spying on other people in their bedrooms. "If it's 'we come in peace', I really don't want to know."

Roselyn traced the letters on the glass. "Write this down quickly, Bet. The ants are leaving and the letters are breaking apart."

Her sister huffed in annoyance but reached for a pen and paper. "L L A B space E H T space Y L N O space L L A M S space K N I H T. Did you get that? It doesn't make sense."

Bet passed the piece of paper to her sister as the last of the ants disappeared into the garden. "You can't expect aliens to write in English!"

"They weren't aliens, they were ants." She snatched the pen from her sister and wrote out the words again, only this time backwards and back to front. "Aha!" she exclaimed, waving the paper in the air. "It's like one of those codes they used in the war – reverse mirror writing. It actually says 'THINK SMALL ONLY THE BALL'."

Bet looked unconvinced. "What type of ball? What would alien ants want with a ball? A nice spot of tennis perhaps!"

But Roselyn had already tuned out her sister's wittering. It was another sign, like the ibis and the paper trail. Killing Cindy was a stupid idea: they just needed to stop her going to the Seniors' Ball. They should be the ones waltzing the night away with Leonard Meeker and collecting tickets for a Caribbean cruise. She knew it – just knew it – somebody or something far greater than their spite was willing them onwards. All they had to do was follow.

⁓

For the next two weeks the sisters did their best to wreck Cindy's chances of attending the Ball. They made sure they were present at all the couple's practice sessions, and sat glaring as they went through their steps.

"Haven't you two witches got anywhere else to be?" snarled

Cindy when Leonard was out of earshot. "Having to look at your repulsive mugs is putting us off our clockwise turns."

"This is the activity room and we are allowed to be here, pursuing quiet activities," replied Bet, thumping a huge pile of crossword puzzles on the table. Roselyn took out the scarf she had started knitting two years ago and thrust the needles upwards as close to Cindy's face as she dared.

On the third day they were moved on by staff, but the waltzers' problems were just beginning. The next morning Cindy's shrieks could be heard throughout Tropical Palms. The hot pink gown she'd chosen for the Ball had been feasted on by silverfish. That afternoon the whole centre went into lockdown after her dancing shoes went missing. Pieces of them were later discovered all over the flowerbeds. However, Cindy's bad luck was miraculously turned around when she found an identical dress and pair of shoes for hire online, and the residents agreed to club together to pay for it.

Roselyn threw her stick across the games room when she found out the good news. "Plagues, pox and pestilence," she spat.

"Well, that may also work," replied a quiet voice.

She looked up to find Mr Tran sitting opposite her in his wheelchair with a benevolent smile on his face. Roselyn's jaw flopped open – she'd never heard him speak before – and his smile grew wider. His eyes glinted in the sun and appeared golden, full of liquid light.

"You won't remember, but I wasn't like this when I first came here," he said, indicating his legs.

Roselyn regarded him with suspicion. "Do you mean you

weren't in that contraption? I'd remember if you'd come skipping into this place. I may be old but I'm not..." Her words trailed off as a series of images filled her head, hazy at first but becoming clear and sharp. She saw Mr Tran walking into Tropical Palms with his son and daughter; got flashes of him playing tennis on the communal court and swimming lengths in the pool. There were glimpses of him playing with energetic grand-children, but then there had been an event, and she suddenly knew it had involved Cindy and those ridiculous bulbous earrings. Except they hadn't always been earrings.

She remembered Mr Tran again, this time holding two crystal marbles, rotating them nimbly between his fingers and carefully, reverentially placing them in a velvet-lined box next to his bed. The vision fast-forwarded until Cindy entered the room, then slipped out with the box. A thief! Roselyn could feel Mr Tran's loss: it was like a slow constriction of breath; the colours of his life seeping away – including his mobility.

When Roselyn broke from the trance her face was wet with tears and Mr Tran was holding on to her hand, his grip icy cold.

"I like to call them the twins of luck and fortune," he said, releasing her hand. "If you choose to believe in such things."

Roselyn rubbed her eyes roughly with the back of her hand. "Utter codswallop and poppycock, as my dear mother used to say."

Despite what she said, her mind raced to other conclusions. It would certainly explain Cindy's run of serendipity. She took a deep breath. "And, if I were to believe in such things..."

"Then you and your sister should think up a new plan," said Mr

Tran smoothly. He turned his wheelchair away and moved slowly towards the glass doors out to the garden. There was a huge, smooth-barked gum tree outside, its branches full of Indian myna birds that gathered in noisy clusters to enjoy the late afternoon sunshine. As Mr Tran approached, the twittering halted abruptly, each bird cocking its tiny head in unison. "You may have to sacrifice what you think you want for what you need to do," he said, pressing one hand against the glass. The birds turned into a flying mass, turning the sky a dark and threatening grey.

⁓⌒⌒⌒

The next morning over coffee and cake, Roselyn announced that she and her sister wouldn't be going to the Ball. Without a hint of sarcasm, she told the gathered residents that they wanted to give "Our wonderful and hard-working staff members the night off to enjoy themselves for a change." The twins were capable and caring individuals, and so had volunteered to look after those residents who couldn't go – like Mr Tran. The hard-working staff spent the rest of the morning sponging stains off the upholstery and sweeping up the gooey remains of dropped Swiss roll.

Cindy's eyebrows practically disappeared into her hairline when she heard the news. "It will give them time to trim their facial hair," she whispered to Leonard as they perfected their left-foot box step.

Finally, the evening of the Ball arrived and the atmosphere at Tropical Palms became electric. As Roselyn sat with her sister and Mr Tran, munching chips in the corner of the communal room, they watched the female residents squeezing themselves into sequinned costumes and stilettos, then applying vast quantities of glittery eye shadow and blush. The air grew stiff with hair spray. Five minutes before the two coaches were due to leave, Cindy and Leonard appeared, wearing matching pumpkin-orange fake tans. They looked like a couple who had already rehearsed their winning smiles.

Cindy motioned for the rest of the women, staff members and Leonard to board the buses, then turned to the corner where the onlookers sat half hidden in the shadows. She absentmindedly played with the glass ball on her right earring, flicking it so it swung like a pendulum. "Enjoy your evening, darlings."

Roselyn swallowed back bile. "You look lovely, Cindy. Bet and I wondered if we could have a photograph with you since we won't be there to see the winning waltz." She spoke with just the right amount of repressed malice to make it believable.

"Why not?" giggled Cindy. "It'll give you something to show your relatives when they come for their annual visit. How do you want me?"

Roselyn willed herself not to say 'dead'.

Bet jumped in. "We've put a star on this door here," she pointed behind her. "Why not stand under it between Roselyn and me. Mr Tran can take the photo."

"Like a rose between two thorny bushes," said Cindy, getting into position, her hands on her hips, elbows pointed out like a teapot.

Mr Tran waved one hand feebly at the women, indicating the mobile phone camera. "He wants you to move back," translated Roselyn. "Your head's not quite under the star."

Cindy took a step backward just as Roselyn pounded her stick violently into the door behind. It shot open and Bet gave Cindy a hard, sharp shove, sending her tumbling through. Bet slammed the door shut and thrust Roselyn's stick behind the handles, locking it. The golden star came fluttering down to reveal a sign underneath:

STORAGE ROOM
Cleaning Supplies

The two sisters walked arm-in-arm to the waiting coaches, telling each driver that Cindy had just boarded the other vehicle.

Back inside the screaming had already started. "You won't get away with this, you evil bitches! How dare you spoil my special night!" The insults flew, along with various implements that pounded into the door, rattling the handles but failing to dislodge Roselyn's stick.

Roselyn took advantage of a momentary pause. "There's no point in screaming like a banshee. None of us are going to the Ball. Might as well shut your trap and sit it out."

Cindy let out a wail, then went quiet. The sisters looked at each other with satisfaction.

"Go and heat up some party pies, Bet," Roselyn instructed. "Might as well enjoy ourselves."

As they munched on their pies, the silence continued, until Roselyn became suspicious. She opened the door just wide enough to switch on the internal lights: there were broken broom handles and puddles of cleaning products but no Cindy. In her smug plotting, Roselyn had forgotten two important facts: Cindy was a fit woman, and she was still wearing the earrings. Luck was on her side. Their eyes followed the teetering tower of boxes and buckets to a skylight. It wasn't very big, but big enough for a yoga-aficionado to escape. All that was left was a single dance shoe, its crystals sparkling in a pool of blue bleach.

Outside a car engine revved up, tyres screeched.

Bet and Roselyn didn't scream, cry or even swear, they simply sagged. Through the open French doors a small wind blew, bringing in fallen gum leaves and bark.

Roselyn lifted her head. "Mr Tran's in the garden, Bet. How did he get..."

Her words trailed off. "Bet! Can you see that? Is it true?"

Mr Tran sat under the gum tree, lifting and swinging his arms in elegant arcs that matched the direction and power of the wind. Tiny pinpricks of light shot between branches like fireflies, darting this way and that, eventually hovering around his head in a pulsing circle of light.

The sisters shuffled into the garden. "Are you a saint then?" asked Roselyn, finally finding her voice. He shook his head and brought his arms down to rest in his lap. The wind stopped immediately.

"We've got lots of work to do to get you to the Ball – we must move fast," he said. "Bring me every curtain you can find, a pair of shoes each and the last of the party pies."

"I was enjoying those," grumbled Bet.

"Do as the man says!" Roselyn snapped, already pulling curtains from their poles. Five minutes later a small pile of floral material lay in front of Mr Tran's chair, along with two pairs of hideous brown sandals and four meat pies.

"He's bloody mad – anyone can see that," said Bet.

But Roselyn didn't answer; she was staring at the line of blinking lights. They had moved from Mr Tran's head to gather around the curtains. As the sisters watched, the lights transformed them into shimmering gold and green fabric which began wrapping around the women in a whirl of complex folds and pleats, compressing their ageing lumps and bumps into shapely curves. Their sandals morphed into jade dancing brogues, which slipped on to their feet.

Mr Tran looked them up and down. "Well, it will have to do," he concluded with a shrug. "To solve the transport problem, I will call on the only real friends I have left." He gathered the remaining the lights in his cupped hands and flung them into the branches above. At once the tree was filled with the noise and movement of creatures: Indian myna birds, locusts and cockroaches flew out of the shadows in rippling swarms, while rats, rabbits and possums scurried down the trunk and through the roots towards them. Several cane toads and snakes emerged from the grass, and four ibis landed beside Mr Tran, snapping up the last of the party pies.

"Well, now I've seen everything!" exclaimed Roselyn.

Mr Tran shook his head. "Not quite."

The gathered creatures began to cluster together into the shape of a car, moving bodies becoming the rounded bumper, fenders, windscreen and wheels of a vehicle. The sisters had shielded their eyes from the flashing golden light, and they blinked in amazement when they saw the Kombi campervan parked beneath the gum tree. Mr Tran slumped down in his chair, eyes closed, chest heaving in and out.

"Well, I guess I'm driving," said Roselyn, throwing her stick into the bushes. "Bet, help me roll the old fellow into the van. We've got a dancing competition to destroy."

Roselyn pulled the handbrake hard; skid marks appeared on the tarmac and the rear wheels leached smoke. She turned to her passengers and gave them the thumbs up. "Hotter than a rev head at Bathurst."

Bet didn't reply, but Roselyn noticed her hands were still gripping the handle bars of the wheelchair. Mr Tran's face was ghostly white, his head bent low over his chest. He had been mumbling something as they drove, and she bent close to hear.

"What's he saying Bet?"

"Something about midnight and breaking spell, or maybe faking smell?"

"Making hell probably, and that's exactly what we're going to do", concluded Roselyn, pushing the wheelchair off the van and through double doors marked 'Emergency Exit'. A piercing alarm sounded, announcing their entrance.

Every person in the dance hall turned, the happy smiles sliding off their faces. There was only one couple on the dance floor: Cindy and Leonard. Their necks twisted at grotesque angles as they tried to hold their positions. A pre-recorded voice suddenly began to blast from speakers around the room, counting down the seconds to midnight.

Then the laughter started. Roselyn glanced down and realised why: their magically fashioned outfits had turned back into curtains and fallen around their ankles, leaving them standing in saggy grey underwear and sandals.

Cindy smiled serenely. She took Leonard by the arm and led him towards the golden gong, secure in her victory.

Without warning, there was a cacophony of animal calls from outside, quickly followed by screams and the noise of rushing bodies. Furry, scaled and winged creatures raced at their unsuspecting prey.

A furious procession of rodents swept Cindy and Leonard off their feet where they lay stunned on the floor, until a flock of ibis dived down, their hooked beaks aimed like arrows at exposed flesh. Roselyn clasped her sister in the eye of the storm of vermin, in a way she hadn't done since they had both been children.

Nobody thought of Mr Tran. (They never did. He had counted on it.) Nobody noticed him except Roselyn. She saw an ibis swoop above his chair, depositing two glass earrings smeared with blood. He rolled them between his hands, a content smile spreading across his face.

And then he stood up.

Inspiration: Cinderella

'Last Man Standing' was inspired by the much-loved fairy tale 'Cinderella'. The story has been given a modern twist by setting the action in Tropical Palms retirement village on the Gold Coast of Australia. Unlike the original tale, this narrative is written from the view point of the 'ugly' sisters, who in this case twin octogenarians Roselyn and Bet. Cindy is far from the downtrodden girl we would recognise in the traditional version of 'Cinderella', but elements of wonder and enchantment still prevail to transport and transform the characters on a magical journey to the Ball.

Author: Claire Hampson

Claire Hampson has been a member of the Northern Beaches Writing Group for over a year now and has found meeting other aspiring and established writers a rewarding experience. She has had a short story published in the 2019 inaugural Arts & Words Project presented as part of the Manly Festival. As a primary school teacher specialising in literacy, Claire has a passion for encouraging children of all ages in their love of reading and writing for pleasure.

Bachorella

Sonia Zadro

Christine's arms ached. She had been holding the boom mic steadily above Judd's thick black hair and aquiline Roman nose for a full fifteen minutes, and there was no end in sight. To make things worse she was still in shock. After three months of working on Season 8 of The Bachelor, her very own stepsister and vanity queen, Vanessa Benson – rebranded as 'Vanessa Starlight' – had ended up as the favourite to win and was currently half naked and draped over Judd's muscular body dressed in a teeny Amazonian bikini for the 'Tarzan and Jane' shoot. Somehow Vanessa, with her sleek blonde hair and sultry poses, had convinced the earnest Judd, that she was not just beautiful, but sweet, if not terribly bright, and that she was one hundred percent committed to finding her soulmate. At this moment Vanessa was trying to achieve this by trailing her fingers along Judd's bare thighs as she rattled on about her career.

"I changed my name of course – a must in the modelling world. It's why I insist people use my full name – it becomes my brand you see? You don't think just 'Marilyn' when you think 'Marilyn Monroe', or 'Cindy' when you think 'Cindy Crawford' do you? That's why I insist. Capiscah?"

Christine noticed Judd frowning in confusion. He wasn't following Vanessa's logic or her dodgy Italian. Glancing down, he seemed more preoccupied with where Vanessa's hands were.

Normally Christine was able to switch off from her sister's vacuous chit chat. Sure, it helped that Judd's broad, muscular chest was on full display, several inches from her face, but being forced to record this sort of rubbish at such close range was making her nauseous. One stepsister on the show was bad enough, but eighteen months ago both her stepsisters applied for the show at the urging of her stepmother; Cliva to promote her make up company 'See All of Me', and Vanessa to promote her modelling career. Back then, her stepmother and stepsisters were furious Christine had scored a job on the set of The Bachelor in pre-production, connecting her with glamorous reality T.V. show stars. Glamorous my ass, Christine thought. Right now, her arms were screaming in pain and her sister was so annoying she felt like dropping the mic, hard, on her head.

Christine glanced over at her other sister Cliva, who was watching the spectacle unfold offset with the other bachelorettes. Cliva's face was as red as one of her overpriced lipsticks and her big blue eyes glared at Vanessa's hand now ominously close to Judd's groin. Christine knew what was coming. Cliva always developed a crick in her neck when she was about to explode. On second thoughts, perhaps having her sisters on set would be more entertaining than she had anticipated?

Suddenly, Vanessa dived in for a full mouth kiss and the scene veered straight out of G into the M+ zone. Judd's flimsy Tarzan pants slipped from one hip, his tackle obscured solely by the angle of Vanessa's thigh draped luxuriously across his leg.

Christine forced herself to keep holding the boom mic. It was her job to capture every moan, every whispered exclamation and every slurp. Anything too disgusting could be edited in post-production. Vanessa's hand inched closer to Judd's tackle and Cliva took the bait.

"Fucking slut!" Cliva screamed. "She's almost rooting him for Christ's sake!"

Christine could just imagine Cliva's foul-mouthed outburst playing over and over again in the ad breaks, with the swearing beeped out of course.

Christine glanced apprehensively at director, Gerard Doyle. Judd and Vanessa were going to land themselves in R rated territory soon. Either that or Cliva was going to punch Vanessa in the face. Should she do something? Finally, Gerard cleared his throat.

"Cut!" he yelled.

"Thank God," muttered Christine. Exhausted, she let her arms drop heavily to her sides. Unfortunately, the corner of her mic snagged Vanessa's bikini, or rather – nipple coverings – on the way down, exposing her perfect silicon C breasts.

Vanessa squealed and laughed, covering her breasts, very slowly Christine noticed, giving Judd a full frontal in the process. Vanessa then muttered to Christine on the side. "Watch it, clutz. Do your job will you!"

Judd frowned and stroked Vanessa's arm, attempting to calm her down. "Are you okay, Vanessa Starlight?"

Vanessa's face slowly returned to a pinker tone and she smiled at Judd, lowering her lashes and giggling. "Forgive me. I'm so nervous. It's all the chemistry between us." Vanessa giggled again fixing her bikini. "I never lose it like that. I'm so sorry, Catrina. Though please remember to say my name properly, it's 'Vanessa Starlight."

Christina internally rolled her eyes. Likewise, she thought, it's Christina, not Catrina. I'm your sister, remember?

"Yes, well anyway," Vanessa continued huskily, as she leant in closer to Judd, and his eyes once again, glazed over. "I'd love to spend more time with you, Judd."

Christine glanced at the other Bachelorettes huddled behind the camera crew and smiled to herself. I guess she'll get what's coming to her with that lot.

Judd pulled himself away with a visible effort and cleared his throat. "Yes, er, perhaps we can talk tonight at the mansion before the rose ceremony?"

"I'll look forward to it." Vanessa beamed at him, her brightest, whitest smile and extracted herself from his lap. She sauntered away to her room with Cliva, hot on her heels, glaring at her from behind.

Judd appeared slightly bewildered. It's amazing what a woman, virtually naked in a bikini could do to a man's frontal lobes. He quickly adjusted his tackle and made himself decent. Christine couldn't help but look at him. Who wouldn't appreciate such a fine specimen of manhood? Bachelors on previous series had always seemed so full of their own importance, and not terribly switched on when it came to discerning the difference between a basically nice, interesting woman from a raging narcissist. The previous display was another example of this and a disappointment to Christine. She really hoped Judd could have seen through her sister. And yet she still liked the guy. Muscles aside somehow she sensed there was a lot more to him. And there had been those occasional moments when he had looked at her so intently she had to look away.

"Hey Christine," he said. "I completely forgot you were Vanessa and Cliva's sister? That must be awkward. Watching your sister make out next to you. I hope you didn't feel too uncomfortable?"

Christine was taken aback. It was the first time Judd had spoken to her. In fact, men in general rarely gave her a second glance with her pale complexion, short spikey brown hair and full figure, which she always hid beneath baggy jeans and a huge t-shirt.

"Oh? It's okay. I mean, it's no weirder then having anyone make out a metre from my face I guess," Christine laughed awkwardly. "Just part of the job."

Judd grinned. "I guess so. Still I didn't like how she spoke to you back there. Sometimes it's hard to tell who's genuine and who isn't on this show."

Christine wondered how much she should reveal. Part of her wanted to grab Judd by the shoulders and scream, 'Run, run, run you fool! She'll screw you for everything you've got!'

Instead she stopped herself and glanced away. "I've barely seen my stepsisters over the past ten years anyway, I hardly know them. Other than Christmas, our stepmother's birthday, that kind of thing. I moved out when I was fifteen for my TAFE diploma in film and TV. Pretty much lived on my own since then."

"Was that hard? Leaving home so young?"

"It was great," she smiled. "I finally had so much freedom."

Christine glanced across and noticed Judd was staring at her with that intense look again. She cleared her throat and looked away.

"Ah... so, only five contestants left." She smiled playfully. "Any idea yet who you're going to pick? Only three weeks before the big finale."

"I'm beginning to wonder if it's possible. I mean it's crazy isn't it, thinking you can find a long-term relationship on a polygamous dating reality show."

Christine couldn't agree more, but bit her tongue. "That's part of the deal though isn't it – to find your life partner, or a serious contender? Unless you're just here to promote your chiropractor business?"

"I hope you're not serious?" he said, offended.

"Umm no, it's just that I know some people who come on the show for... personal reasons." She took a deep breath. "So anyway, why are you here if not to meet Mrs Right?"

Judd ran his fingers through his hair. "If you really want to know the truth, I was not having much luck on my own."

"Seriously? You're telling me it's difficult for you to find women to date?" Christine raised her eyebrows.

"Yes." Judd glanced at her and looked away. "I can get pretty anxious about dating and hoped this would help."

Christine couldn't contain herself and released a giggle.

For a moment, Judd didn't reply. He seemed pensive, sad.

Christine frowned. "Hey I'm sorry. I didn't mean to offend you."

Judd frowned. "Yeah, well, I'll remember that next time. The thing is, if you can't relax and be yourself on a date, the relationship doesn't get very far."

Before Christine could respond sympathetically, they were interrupted by their director, Gerard,

"Judd!" Gerard was pacing frantically back and forth. "Get to your bachelor pad and clean up for tonight's rose ceremony! Christine, I want you in the Green Room. Emergency meeting now."

"Me? Why me?"

"Green room! I'll explain in a minute."

When she reached the Green Room, Gerard nodded to the producer, Mannie Rose who came straight to the point.

"The Intruders have quit. They're leaving first thing in the morning."

Christine's mouth fell open. The Intruders were due to go on set tonight. "Didn't they sign a contract, Mannie? What happened?"

"They refuse to be on camera under false pretences and they don't care about the money they'll lose"

"What are you talking about?" asked Christine.

"They found love with each other, apparently," interrupted Gerard.

"They were only shown to their room three days ago?" continued Christine.

"Yes, their room, and their bed," continued Mannie, "the one they shared."

Gerard was starting to sweat. "I don't want to talk about those bloody lesbian Intruders. We need at least one Intruder to go on set as per the schedule tonight."

Gerard cleared his throat. "Christine... we need you, you're our only hope."

'I'm what?"

"You're our only hope, you're the Intruder!"

Christine stared at Gerard. She was speechless.

"It's why I asked you here. We're desperate. You're the only female member of the crew who's the right age, even if you are no beauty queen."

Christine rolled her eyes, "Thanks."

"Christine please. It's just for one night. You'll be all done, off set and back to plain Jane by midnight. I want you back operating that boom tomorrow. No one will even know it's you – we'll make you incognito and have Judd throw you out at the rose ceremony tonight." Gerard ran his hand through his hair and pulled it along its length.

The thought of facing her sisters on national television made her stomach churn but she wanted to help Gerard out. And what was one night?

"Alright then. I'll do it. As long as no one can recognise me."

Gerard released a breath. "Wonderful. Now straight to hair and make-up. Manu will see to that."

⁀◦⸺◦⸽

Two hours later, after a head-to-toe massage, full body wax, manicure, pedicure, facial cleanse, mask and moisturiser, Christine lay back thinking it was all worth it, just for how she was feeling right now. A shrill voice interrupted her bliss.

"Sweetings! Sweetings! Tell me she is all ready?"

Christine opened one eye and saw someone tall, beautiful, and blonde, heavily made-up and in a long white dress. She opened her other eye and noticed a pair of large muscular arms and an Adam's apple – a tall beautiful blond man.

Manu leaned over Christine and smiled down at her.

Christine smiled awkwardly back. "Hi. Ahh… who are you?"

"Me? Why didn't Gerard tell you? I'm your fairy godmother sweetheart, come to make you into a princess. You may call me Manu. Oh and such a canvas. Fine strong lines, such untapped potential. Let me look at you." Manu held her cheek gently and turned her face from one side to the other. "I can't wait. What colour do you usually wear, sweeting?"

"Oh. Black, I guess."

"Ah!" Manu screamed and Christine jumped. "Black is all wrong for you with your colouring. Let's go for a rich red – fire engine please – to bring out those big chocolate eyes, long lashes and that creamy white skin. Hair extensions? Yes, long dark chestnut ones, and a long slit in the dress please, she has stunning legs! Girls, quick sticks! We want to make him fall in love with her and have all the Godzillas writhing in jealousy."

Christine was so in awe of this beautiful transvestite that she didn't have the heart to insist she wouldn't make any man fall in love with her with make-up and a nice dress, especially for the finely chiselled Judd. Men didn't notice her curvy looks, spikey dark hair, and slightly hooked nose. She had always been referred to by her sisters as their Greek piggy as they ordered her around, since she had taken after her late mother's dark looks. In fact her sisters taunts had made her feel so ashamed she always hid her looks under baggy clothes.

Cliva and Vanessa on the other hand were fair, tall and blonde like their mother, who had married their father when Christine was five. Regardless she may as well lap up the attention. After all it was free and the only time she was likely to experience such an indulgence.

Three hours later, Christine was staring at a beautiful woman with gleaming long, wavy brown tresses, smouldering dark eyes, and red lips in a dress that dipped low at her full round breasts, flattered her wide hips, and showed off her long shapely legs. God, she was unrecognisable and this stranger was stunning.

"Wow."

Manu was clasping her hands with tears in her eyes, muttering. "Writhing in jealousy those Godzillas. What did I say!"

"I even look thin! For me that is."

"Magic underwear and the right shape dress go a long way, sweeting." Manu turned to Christine and looked her straight in the eye. "But it's all you. Don't you forget it."

That's not me, Christine thought. But she was happy to pretend for the night.

Manu leaned over and kissed her. "Now go get them, sweeting. Go get them."

The five remaining bachelorettes were huddled together by the pool with Judd, vying for his attention, when Christine walked up to them. She was so sick with nerves she could barely speak. With hands shaking, palms slick with sweat, and her heart hammering she attempted to introduce herself.

"Hi," she squeaked.

All the Bachelorettes stopped speaking and stared. Judd appeared speechless.

Cliva broke the silence. "So you're the Intruder everyone's been talking about?"

Christine's mouth went dry and she nodded.

Cliva laughed. "And do you have a name?"

Christine couldn't do this. She froze and glanced at Cliva's drink. "Brandy," she said, "Brandy White."

"You look like you need one," interjected Vanessa, picking up the drink she had clearly half finished. "Here, take mine I haven't even taken a sip."

"Um, would you like to have a chat, Brandy?" Judd finally found his tongue. He was staring at her with clear interest but there was also kindness in his eyes. He could see how uncomfortable she was.

He gently led her away from the other girls around the side of the mansion, to an undercover gazebo. Here large pink proteas, red grevilleas, yellow wattle and kangaroo paw lined the white circular structure. Jasmine was twined through the roof, hanging down in places to touch the floor, surrounding them with white flowers and a heavenly scent.

Judd guided her to a seat with soft reclining cushions and

champagne on a small table nearby. There were two discrete cameras pitched on the top of the gazebo.

"Feeling better?" he asked.

"Thanks. Umm I've never been on camera before."

"Me neither before this show. I know what it feels like to get anxious."

Christine almost laughed but caught herself this time. "You seem pretty confident."

"I know," Judd glanced away. "I don't usually talk about it but I used to have an anxiety problem as a teenager. Basically I was really shy. Had to see a shrink and everything. It was really debilitating."

"Wow. That sounds bad?"

Judd grimaced. "Worse. But after years of therapy and forcing myself to face my fears, I've come a long way."

Christine thought of her sisters and how hard it had always been to stand up to them. "I wish I was that courageous. I mean in facing my fears."

"Of course you can, Brandy. You just need to take it slowly. That's what I learnt anyway."

Christine looked up at him. "Hey, thanks for being so open."

Judd reached out for her hand and stroked it. Christine felt a rush of electricity at his touch. "You have a heart shaped birth-mark on your wrist," he said with a smile.

Christine blushed. "I always try to hide it. It's kind of ugly."

To her surprise he brought her wrist to his mouth and gently kissed it. "It's not ugly. Not at all."

He had that kind look in his green eyes again. Then he

glanced over her dress and his look became more heated. "I feel pretty comfortable with you, Brandy. I'm not usually one to share much actually. You have no idea how glad I am that you were the Intruder tonight."

Christine's breath hitched. She was so attracted to him and couldn't seem to look away from his eyes. Judd leaned closer, it seemed almost involuntarily. His ran his hand along her arm and leaned in brushing his lips along hers. His tongue flicked out along her bottom lip and Christine responded. Energy vibrated through her body and she pressed herself up against his chest. Their kiss deepened and seemed to last a long time until Judd moved back and cleared his throat.

"I hope you didn't mind that."

Christine stared up at him with a glazed look in her eyes. "No."

"I mean I'm not usually that forward."

"I know..." Christine caught herself. Having been on set for three months she knew he had only kissed three girls this season. "I mean, you don't seem like you're usually that forward."

"It's just, I mean... I'd just, I'd really like to get to know you better, Brandy."

Christine looked at his beautiful kind green eyes. "I'd like to get to know you better too."

Judd smiled. Then he rummaged behind the seats and to her astonishment held out a rose to her.

"Brandy, will you accept this rose."

Christine panicked. She was meant to be leaving by midnight so she could continue working the boom for the rest of this season's shoot, but she didn't want to hurt Judd's feelings. "Oh, of course," she mumbled.

The moment was interrupted by a shrill scream echoing across the entire resort.

"Aaaaaaaaaaah!"

Christine would have recognised Cliva's squeal anywhere and it was followed by her usual pattern of hysterics.

"Bloody slut! Only an hour and you've hooked him line and sinker! Where did they dig you up from anyway? We just overheard Oscher tell the producer the two real Intruders went leso and did a runner. Who are you, Brandy?"

Christine backed away, but Judd stepped in front of her.

"Control yourself, Cliva. Obviously she is an Intruder as well. Apologise to Brandy."

Cliva glared at Judd and her face went red. "Apologise? Apologise?" she shrieked. She stormed past Judd and shoved Christine into the nearby grevillea bush. Christine fell back into it and snagged her dress on a branch, which dug into her hip. Her arms and legs were splayed as she struggled to find her feet. She was just envisioning the close up on camera and she prayed no one would recognise her.

Judd turned to Cliva, furious. He spoke softly. "Leave. Now."

Christine felt tears welling up. No one in her life had ever defended her.

Cliva stepped backwards scowling. "Fine!" She spun on her heals and stormed off.

Christine feared her tears would spill at any moment. She had to get away. "Thanks, Judd. I think I'll just go and fix my dress."

She scuttled away quickly knowing she wouldn't be at the rose ceremony tonight. She just hoped Judd would forgive her.

Three weeks later, Christine was once again holding the boom mic several inches from Judd's handsome face. It was the final scene in The Bachelor's finale. Judd hadn't coped well when Brandy had mysteriously disappeared that night just before the rose ceremony. He'd even threatened to quit. But then, quite suddenly, he seemed to have gotten over it. Christine wasn't surprised. She had always known she was the forgettable type. It wasn't like Judd would like her, not looking like this anyway. It would just be another humiliating rejection to add to the long line of rejections in her life.

Right now, however, a worse nightmare was unfolding before her. Judd had just rejected the second last hopeful bachelorette and was about to declare his undying love to the final contestant – her noxious stepsister, Vanessa Starlight.

"Vanessa Starlight, you're an incredibly beautiful woman and you've accomplished so much."

Vanessa smiled smugly. "We were right for each other all along Judd. I could feel it."

"And I'm very attracted to you physically."

"I know, and I you Judd."

"But I'm afraid I'm looking for something else."

"What?"

What, thought Christine. What was he doing? Was this another Nick Cummings double rejection? She could only hope so for Judd's sake.

"Yes. I'm afraid there's been only one woman I've felt a genuine, deep connection with over the past few weeks, and I was so devastated, so worried that I'd lost her."

Judd turned and looked directly at Christine holding the boom. He smiled warmly and lifted his hand to trace the heart shaped birthmark on her wrist. "But I haven't lost her."

Christine stared at him open mouthed and the boom dropped from her hands landing on the floor with a clunk.

"Christine? I know it was you. I was stupid not to see it sooner. I'm sorry."

"No, I… I'm sorry," Christine stammered. "I couldn't tell you the truth or say goodbye."

Judd tenderly moved his hand to trace her jaw.

Vanessa Starlight stared at Judd, confused. Her face was beginning to flush red. "Judd. I'm here. Why are you talking to the help? Stop touching our Greek piggy!"

Christine suddenly felt her blood boil. She turned and glared at her sister. "What did you call me?"

"Your name of course! What is going on here?"

"My name is Christine, Vanessa, and from now on I want you to say it, you cow!"

Judd turned back to Vanessa scowling. "Yes, say it Vanessa and apologise."

Vanessa's face flared bright red and her voice sounded hysterical. "Are you mad! I'm not apologising to Greek piggy! And you are marrying me, Judd!"

Judd turned to Vanessa. "I thought you were a strong, sweet woman. But you're a fake, selfish, bitch Vanessa. And if you don't leave now, I'm demanding security carry you off."

"How dare you!"

Vanessa glared at the two security guards stepping up closer to Judd. She flicked her hair, livid, turned on her heels, and stormed off the set.

Once out of earshot Judd turned to Christine. "If anyone ever insults you like that again I will personally slap them."

Christine couldn't stop the tears streaming down her face. She looked into Judd's kind eyes and smiled. "If anyone insults me again like that, especially one of my stepsisters, I will personally slap them. It's way overdue."

Judd grinned and pulled her close. "I really like you, Christine." Then he got down on one knee and held her hand. "Christine will you please give me the honour of going on a proper date with me?"

"Christine couldn't wipe the smile from her face. "I'd love too."

Judd stood up then and kissed her thoroughly, and Christine kissed him right back.

Inspiration: Cinderella

'Bachorella' is a modern adaptation of the classic fairy tale 'Cinderella' set in a present day reality television hit series similar to 'The Bachelor'. It explores themes of worthiness and desirability common to the modern day woman in a fun light-hearted context.

Of Beasts & Butterflies

Author: Sonia Zadro

Sonia Zadro is a psychologist and freelance magazine writer who has written and published several short stories. Her story 'Oscar' gained highly commended in the 2016 BezerkaCon competition and was published in the anthology 'A Fearsome Engine' (NBWG, 2016), her story 'The Big Dipper' was published in the anthology 'A Noise on an Island' (NBWG, 2018), and '52 Hetz' was recently selected for inclusion in the 2019 Manly Arts Festival's 'Art & Words Project' anthology 'Saltwater' (Northern Beaches Council, 2019).

Acknowledgements

Zena Shapter

Once upon a time fairytales were magical, enchanting tales where anything could happen, and the real world often met the supernatural with a creative spark that captured our imaginations. Often intended for or featuring children, they were handed down from storyteller to storyteller, and many have been adapted and retold countless times.

This anthology is no exception, and I'd like to thank the authors who contributed, for running with my idea to create a broad range of reimagined tales *not* for children! Their generous imaginations, creativity, and collaborative spirit has produced a fascinating and delightful anthology of original, yet familiar stories. Well done!

Thanks also to the editors who gave up their valuable time to read and edit stories, often multiple times: Phil Burgin, Suzi Green, Megan Holbeck, Azmeena Kelly, Joanna Mawson-Lee, Tony McFadden, Mijmark, Tara Ray, Rose Saltman, and Susan Steggall.

Thank you to our exceptional proofreaders who gave up their

valuable time to hunt through the manuscripts for typos: Rodney Jensen, Rebecca King, Campbell McConachie, Tara Ray, Howard Reid, Rose Saltman, Amy Spurling, and Susan Steggall.

Finally, I'm sure everyone would like to thank their friends and families for their support, as I would like to thank mine – your support and acceptance are the backbone to everything I do. You know how I love books!

Zena Shapter
Editor-in-Chief

Also by the
NORTHERN BEACHES WRITERS' GROUP